I0535211

L Frank Baum - The Enchanted Island of Yew

Whereon Prince Marvel Encountered the High Ki of Twi and Other Surprising People

Lyman Frank Baum was born on May 15, 1856 in Chittenango, New York. A sickly child he was schooled at home until the age of 12. He was fascinated by printing and early on was given a printing press from which he produced a number of journals.

In 1880, his father built him a theatre in Richburg, New York, and Baum set about writing plays and gathering together an actor's company. The Maid of Arran, was his first and proved a modest success.

In 1897, he wrote and published Mother Goose in Prose, a collection of Mother Goose rhymes written as prose stories, and illustrated by Maxfield Parrish. It allowed Baum to quit his door-to-door sales job. In 1899 Baum partnered with illustrator W. W. Denslow, to publish Father Goose, His Book, a collection of nonsense poetry was a success, becoming the best-selling children's book of the year.

In 1900, Baum and Denslow published The Wonderful Wizard of Oz to critical acclaim and financial success. It was the best-selling children's book for two years running. Baum went on to write thirteen more novels based on the places and people of the Land of Oz.

On May 5, 1919, Baum suffered from a stroke. He died quietly the next day, nine days short of his 63rd birthday. He was buried in Glendale's Forest Lawn Memorial Park Cemetery.

Index of Contents

Chapter 1 - "Once On a Time"

I am going to tell a story, one of those tales of astonishing adventures that happened years and years and years ago. Perhaps you wonder why it is that so many stories are told of "once on a time", and so few of these days in which we live; but that is easily explained.

In the old days, when the world was young, there were no automobiles nor flying-machines to make one wonder; nor were there railway trains, nor telephones, nor mechanical inventions of any sort to keep people keyed up to a high pitch of excitement. Men and women lived simply and quietly. They were Nature's children, and breathed fresh air into their lungs instead of smoke and coal gas; and tramped through green meadows and deep forests instead of riding in street cars; and went to bed when it grew dark and rose with the sun, which is vastly different from the present custom. Having no books to read they told their adventures to one another and to their little ones; and the stories were handed down from generation to generation and reverently believed.

Those who peopled the world in the old days, having nothing but their hands to depend on, were to a certain extent helpless, and so the fairies were sorry for them and ministered to their wants patiently and frankly, often showing themselves to those they befriended.

So people knew fairies in those days, my dear, and loved them, together with all the ryls and knooks and pixies and nymphs and other beings that belong to the hordes of immortals. And a fairy tale was a thing to be wondered at and spoken of in awed whispers; for no one thought of doubting its truth.

To-day the fairies are shy; for so many curious inventions of men have come into use that the wonders of Fairyland are somewhat tame beside them, and even the boys and girls can not be so easily interested or surprised as in the old days. So the sweet and gentle little immortals perform their tasks unseen and unknown, and live mostly in their own beautiful realms, where they are almost unthought of by our busy, bustling world.

Yet when we come to story-telling the marvels of our own age shrink into insignificance beside the brave deeds and absorbing experiences of the days when fairies were better known; and so we go back to "once on a time" for the tales that we most love and that children have ever loved since mankind knew that fairies exist.

Chapter 2 - The Enchanted Isle

Once there was an enchanted island in the middle of the sea. It was called the Isle of Yew. And in it were five important kingdoms ruled by men, and many woodland dells and forest glades and pleasant meadows and grim mountains inhabited by fairies.

From the fairies some of the men had learned wonderful secrets, and had become magicians and sorcerers, with powers so great that the entire island was reputed to be one of enchantments. Who these men were the common people did not always know; for while some were kings and rulers, others lived quietly hidden away in forests or mountains, and seldom or never showed themselves. Indeed, there were not so many of these magicians as people thought, only it was so hard to tell them from common folk that every stranger was regarded with a certain amount of curiosity and fear.

The island was round, like a mince pie. And it was divided into four Quarters, also like a pie, except that there was a big place in the center where the fifth kingdom, called Spor, lay in the midst of the mountains. Spor was ruled by King Terribus, whom no one but his own subjects had ever seen and not many of them. For no one was allowed to enter the Kingdom of Spor, and its king never left his palace. But the people of Spor had a bad habit of rushing down from their mountains and stealing the goods of the inhabitants of the other four kingdoms, and carrying them home with them, without offering any apologies whatever for such horrid conduct. Sometimes those they robbed tried to fight them; but they were a terrible people, consisting of giants with huge clubs, and dwarfs who threw flaming darts, and the stern Gray Men of Spor, who were most frightful of all. So, as a rule, every one fled before them, and the people were thankful that the fierce warriors of Spor seldom came to rob them oftener than once a year.

It was on this account that all who could afford the expense built castles to live in, with stone walls so thick that even the giants of Spor could not batter them down. And the children were not allowed to stray far from home for fear some roving band of robbers might steal them and make their parents pay large sums for their safe return.

Yet for all this the people of the Enchanted Isle of Yew were happy and prosperous. No grass was greener, no forests more cool and delightful, no skies more sunny, no sea more blue and rippling than theirs.

And the nations of the world envied them, but dared not attempt to conquer an island abounding in enchantments.

Chapter 3 - The Fairy Bower

That part of the Enchanted Isle which was kissed by the rising sun was called Dawna; the kingdom that was tinted rose and purple by the setting sun was known as Auriel, and the southland, where fruits and flowers abounded, was the kingdom of Plenta. Up at the north lay Heg, the home of the great barons who feared not even the men of Spor; and in the Kingdom of Heg our story opens.

Upon a beautiful plain stood the castle of the great Baron Merd, renowned alike in war and peace, and second in importance only to the King of Heg. It was a castle of vast extent, built with thick walls and protected by strong gates. In front of it sloped a pretty stretch of land with the sea glistening far beyond; and back of it, but a short distance away, was the edge of the Forest of Lurla.

One fair summer day the custodian of the castle gates opened a wicket and let down a draw-bridge, when out trooped three pretty girls with baskets dangling on their arms. One of the maids walked in front of her companions, as became the only daughter of the mighty Baron Merd. She was named Seseley, and had yellow hair and red cheeks and big, blue eyes. Behind her, merry and laughing, yet with a distinct deference to the high station of their young lady, walked Berna and Helda, dark brunettes with mischievous eyes and slender, lithe limbs. Berna was the daughter of the chief archer, and Helda the niece of the captain of the guard, and they were appointed play-fellows and comrades of the fair Seseley.

Up the hill to the forest's edge ran the three, and then without hesitation plunged into the shade of the ancient trees. There was no sunlight now, but the air was cool and fragrant of nuts and mosses, and the children skipped along the paths joyously and without fear.

To be sure, the Forest of Lurla was well known as the home of fairies, but Seseley and her comrades feared nothing from such gentle creatures and only longed for an interview with the powerful immortals whom they had been taught to love as the tender guardians of mankind. Nymphs there were in Lurla, as well, and crooked knooks, it was said; yet for many years past no person could boast the favor of meeting any one of the fairy creatures face to face.

So, gathering a few nuts here and a sweet forest flower there, the three maidens walked farther and farther into the forest until they came upon a clearing, formed like a circle, with mosses and ferns for its carpet and great overhanging branches for its roof.

"How pretty!" cried Seseley, gaily. "Let us eat our luncheon in this lovely banquet-hall!"

So Berna and Helda spread a cloth and brought from their baskets some golden platters and a store of food. Yet there was little ceremony over the meal, you may be sure, and within a short space all the children had satisfied their appetites and were laughing and chatting as merrily as if they were at home in the great castle. Indeed, it is certain they were happier in their forest glade than when facing grim walls of stone, and the three were in such gay spirits that whatever one chanced to say the others promptly joined in laughing over.

Soon, however, they were startled to hear a silvery peal of laughter answering their own, and turning to see whence the sound proceeded, they found seated near them a creature so beautiful that at once the three pairs of eyes opened to their widest extent, and three hearts beat much faster than before.

"Well, I must say you DO stare!" exclaimed the newcomer, who was clothed in soft floating robes of rose and pearl color, and whose eyes shone upon them like two stars.

"Forgive our impertinence," answered the little Lady Seseley, trying to appear dignified and unmoved; "but you must acknowledge that you came among us uninvited, and, and you are certainly rather odd in appearance."

Again the silvery laughter rang through the glade.

"Uninvited!" echoed the creature, clapping her hands together delightedly; "uninvited to my own forest home! Why, my dear girls, you are the uninvited ones, indeed you are, to thus come romping into our fairy bower."

The children did not open their eyes any wider on hearing this speech, for they could not; but their faces expressed their amazement fully, while Helda gasped the words:

"A fairy bower! We are in a fairy bower!"

"Most certainly," was the reply. "And as for being odd in appearance, let me ask how you could reasonably expect a fairy to appear as mortal maidens do?"

"A fairy!" exclaimed Seseley. "Are you, then, a real fairy?"

"I regret to say I am," returned the other, more soberly, as she patted a moss-bank with a silver-tipped wand.

Then for a moment there was silence, while the three girls sat very still and stared at their immortal companion with evident curiosity. Finally Seseley asked:

"Why do you regret being a fairy? I have always thought them the happiest creatures in the world."

"Perhaps we ought to be happy," answered the fairy, gravely, "for we have wonderful powers and do much to assist you helpless mortals. And I suppose some of us really are happy. But, for my part, I am so utterly tired of a fairy life that I would do anything to change it."

"That is strange," declared Berna. "You seem very young to be already discontented with your lot."

Now at this the fairy burst into laughter again, and presently asked:

"How old do you think me?"

"About our own age," said Berna, after a glance at her and a moment's reflection.

"Nonsense!" retorted the fairy, sharply. "These trees are hundreds of years old, yet I remember when they were mere twigs. And I remember when mortals first came to live upon this island, yes and when this island was first created and rose from the sea after a great earthquake. I remember for many, many centuries, my dears. I have grown tired of remembering and of being a fairy continually, without any change to brighten my life."

"To be sure!" said Seseley, with sympathy. "I never thought of fairy life in that way before. It must get to be quite tiresome."

"And think of the centuries I must yet live!" exclaimed the fairy in a dismal voice. "Isn't it an awful thing to look forward to?"

"It is, indeed," agreed Seseley.

"I'd be glad to exchange lives with you," said Helda, looking at the fairy with intense admiration.

"But you can't do that," answered the little creature quickly. "Mortals can't become fairies, you know, although I believe there was once a mortal who was made immortal."

"But fairies can become anything they desire!" cried Berna.

"Oh, no, they can't. You are mistaken if you believe that," was the reply. "I could change YOU into a fly, or a crocodile, or a bobolink, if I wanted to; but fairies can't change themselves into anything else."

"How strange!" murmured Seseley, much impressed.

"But YOU can," cried the fairy, jumping up and coming toward them. "You are mortals, and, by the laws that govern us, a mortal can change a fairy into anything she pleases."

"Oh!" said Seseley, filled with amazement at the idea.

The fairy fell on her knees before the baron's daughter. "Please, please, dear Seseley," she pleaded, "change me into a mortal!"

Chapter 4 - Prince Marvel

It is easy to imagine the astonishment of the three girls at hearing this strange request. They gazed in a bewildered fashion upon the kneeling fairy, and were at first unable to answer one word. Then Seseley said sadly, for she grieved to disappoint the pretty creature:

"We are but mortal children, and have no powers of enchantment at all."

"Ah, that is true, so far as concerns yourselves," replied the fairy, eagerly; "yet mortals may easily transform fairies into anything they wish."

"If that is so, why have we never heard of this power before?" asked Seseley.

"Because fairies, as a rule, are content with their lot, and do not wish to appear in any form but their own. And, knowing that evil or mischievous mortals can transform them at will, the fairies take great care to remain invisible, so they can not be interfered with. Have you ever," she asked, suddenly, "seen a fairy before?"

"Never," replied Seseley.

"Nor would you have seen me to-day, had I not known you were kind and pure-hearted, or had I not resolved to ask you to exercise your powers upon me."

"I must say," remarked Helda, boldly, "that you are foolish to wish to become anything different from what you are."

"For you are very beautiful NOW," added Berna, admiringly.

"Beautiful!" retorted the fairy, with a little frown; "what does beauty amount to, if one is to remain invisible?"

"Not much, that is true," agreed Berna, smoothing her own dark locks.

"And as for being foolish," continued the fairy, "I ought to be allowed to act foolishly if I want to. For centuries past I have not had a chance to do a single foolish thing."

"Poor dear!" said Helda, softly.

Seseley had listened silently to this conversation. Now she inquired:

"What do you wish to become?"

"A mortal!" answered the fairy, promptly.

"A girl, like ourselves?" questioned the baron's daughter.

"Perhaps," said the fairy, as if undecided.

"Then you would be likely to endure many privations," said Seseley, gently. "For you would have neither father nor mother to befriend you, nor any house to live in."

"And if you hired your services to some baron, you would be obliged to wash dishes all day, or mend clothing, or herd cattle," said Berna.

"But I should travel all over the island," said the fairy, brightly, "and that is what I long to do. I do not care to work."

"I fear a girl would not be allowed to travel alone," Seseley remarked, after some further thought. "At least," she added, "I have never heard of such a thing."

"No," said the fairy, rather bitterly, "your men are the ones that roam abroad and have adventures of all kinds. Your women are poor, weak creatures, I remember."

There was no denying this, so the three girls sat silent until Seseley asked:

"Why do you wish to become a mortal?"

"To gain exciting experiences," answered the fairy. I'm tired of being a humdrum fairy year in and year out. Of course, I do not wish to become a mortal for all time, for that would get monotonous, too; but to live a short while as the earth people do would amuse me very much."

"If you want variety, you should become a boy," said Helda, with a laugh, "The life of a boy is one round of excitement."

"Then make me a boy!" exclaimed the fairy eagerly.

"A boy!" they all cried in consternation. And Seseley added:

"Why, you're a GIRL fairy, aren't you?"

"Well, yes; I suppose I am," answered the beautiful creature, smiling; "but as you are going to change me anyway, I may as well become a boy as a girl."

"Better!" declared Helda, clapping her hands; "for then you can do as you please."

"But would it be right?" asked Seseley, with hesitation.

"Why not?" retorted the fairy. "I can see nothing wrong in being a boy. Make me a tall, slender youth, with waving brown hair and dark eyes. Then I shall be as unlike my own self as possible, and the adventure will be all the more interesting. Yes; I like the idea of being a boy very much indeed."

"But I don't know how to transform you; some one will have to show me the way to do it," protested Seseley, who was getting worried over the task set her.

"Oh, that will be easy enough," returned the little immortal. "Have you a wand?"

"No."

"Then I'll loan you mine, for I shall not need it. And you must wave it over my head three times and say: 'By my mortal powers I transform you into a boy for the space of one year'."

"One year! Isn't that too long?"

"It's a very short time to one who has lived thousands of years as a fairy."

"That is true," answered the baron's daughter.

"Now, I'll begin by doing a little transforming myself," said the fairy, getting upon her feet again, "and you can watch and see how I do it." She brushed a bit of moss from her gauzy skirts and continued: "If I'm to become a boy I shall need a horse, you know. A handsome, prancing steed, very fleet of foot."

A moment she stood motionless, as if listening. Then she uttered a low but shrill whistle.

The three girls, filled with eager interest, watched her intently.

Presently a trampling of footsteps was heard through the brushwood, and a beautiful deer burst from the forest and fearlessly ran to the fairy. Without hesitation she waved her wand above the deer's head and exclaimed:

"By all my fairy powers I command you to become a war-horse for the period of one year."

Instantly the deer disappeared, and in its place was a handsome charger, milk-white in color, with flowing mane and tail. Upon its back was a saddle sparkling with brilliant gems sewn upon fine dressed leather.

The girls uttered cries of astonishment and delight, and the fairy said:

"You see, these transformations are not at all difficult. I must now have a sword."

She plucked a twig from a near-by tree and cast it upon the ground at her feet. Again she waved her wand and the twig turned to a gleaming sword, richly engraved, that seemed to the silent watchers to tremble slightly in its sheath, as if its heart of steel throbbed with hopes of battles to come.

"And now I must have shield and armor, said the fairy, gaily. "This will make a shield," and she stripped a sheet of loose bark from a tree-trunk, "but for armor I must have something better. Will you give me your cloak?"

This appeal was made to Seseley, and the baron's daughter drew her white velvet cloak from her shoulders and handed it to the fairy. A moment later it was transformed into a suit of glittering armor that seemed fashioned of pure silver inlaid with gold, while the sheet of bark at the same time became a handsome shield, with the figures of three girls graven upon it. Seseley recognized the features as those of herself and her comrades, and noted also that they appeared sitting at the edge of a forest, the great trees showing plainly in the background.

"I shall be your champion, you see," laughed the fairy, gleefully, "and maybe I shall be able to repay you for the loss of your cloak."

"I do not mind the cloak," returned the child, who had been greatly interested in these strange transformations. "But it seems impossible that a dainty little girl like you can ride this horse and carry these heavy arms."

"I'll not be a girl much longer," said the little creature. "Here, take my wand, and transform me into a noble youth!"

Again the pretty fairy knelt before Seseley, her dainty, rounded limbs of white and rose showing plainly through her gauzy attire. And the baron's daughter was suddenly inspired to be brave, not wishing to disappoint the venturous immortal. So she rose and took the magic wand in her hand, waving it three times above the head of the fairy.

"By my powers as a mortal," she said, marveling even then at the strange speech, "I command you to become a brave and gallant youth; handsome, strong, fearless! And such shall you remain for the space of one year.

As she ceased speaking the fairy was gone, and a slender youth, dark-eyed and laughing, was holding her hand in his and kissing it gratefully.

"I thank you, most lovely maiden," he said, in a pleasant voice, "for giving me a place in the world of mortals. I shall ride at once in search of adventure, but my good sword is ever at your service."

With this he gracefully arose and began to buckle on his magnificent armor and to fasten the sword to his belt.

Seseley drew a long, sighing breath of amazement at her own powers, and turning to Berna and Helda she asked:

"Do I see aright? Is the little fairy really transformed to this youth?"

"It certainly seems so," returned Helda, who, being unabashed by the marvels she had beheld, turned to gaze boldly upon the young knight.

"Do you still remember that a moment ago you were a fairy?" she inquired.

"Yes, indeed," said he, smiling; "and I am really a fairy now, being but changed in outward form. But no one must know this save yourselves, until the year has expired and I resume my true station. Will you promise to guard my secret?"

"Oh, yes!" they exclaimed, in chorus. For they were delighted, as any children might well be, at having so remarkable a secret to keep and talk over among themselves.

"I must ask one more favor," continued the youth: "that you give me a name; for in this island I believe all men bear names of some sort, to distinguish them one from another."

"True," said Seseley, thoughtfully. "What were you called as a fairy?"

"That does not matter in the least," he answered, hastily. "I must have an entirely new name."

"Suppose we call him the Silver Knight," suggested Berna, as she eyed his glistening armor.

"Oh, no! that is no name at all!" declared Helda. "We might better call him Baron Strongarm."

"I do not like that, either," said the Lady Seseley, "for we do not know whether his arm is strong or not. But he has been transformed in a most astonishing and bewildering manner before our very eyes, and I think the name of Prince Marvel would suit him very well."

"Excellent!" cried the youth, picking up his richly graven shield. "The name seems fitting in every way. And for a year I shall be known to all this island as Prince Marvel!"

Chapter 5 - The King of Thieves

Old Marshelm, the captain of the guard, was much surprised when he saw the baron's daughter and her playmates approach her father's castle escorted by a knight in glittering armor.

To be sure it was a rather small knight, but the horse he led by the bridle was so stately and magnificent in appearance that old Marshelm, who was an excellent judge of horses, at once decided the stranger must be a personage of unusual importance.

As they came nearer the captain of the guard also observed the beauty of the little knight's armor, and caught the glint of jewels set in the handle of his sword; so he called his men about him and prepared to receive the knight with the honors doubtless due his high rank.

But to the captain's disappointment the stranger showed no intention of entering the castle. On the contrary, he kissed the little Lady Seseley's hand respectfully, waved an adieu to the others, and then mounted his charger and galloped away over the plains.

The drawbridge was let down to permit the three children to enter, and the great Baron Merd came himself to question his daughter.

"Who was the little knight?" he asked.

"His name is Prince Marvel," answered Seseley, demurely.

"Prince Marvel?" exclaimed the Baron. "I have never heard of him. Does he come from the Kingdom of Dawna, or that of Auriel, or Plenta?"

"That I do not know," said Seseley, with truth.

"Where did you meet him?" continued the baron.

"In the forest, my father, and he kindly escorted us home."

"Hm!" muttered the baron, thoughtfully. "Did he say what adventure brought him to our Kingdom of Heg?"

"No, father. But he mentioned being in search of adventure."

"Oh, he'll find enough to busy him in this wild island, where every man he meets would rather draw his sword than eat," returned the old warrior, smiling. "How old may this Prince Marvel be?"

"He looks not over fifteen years of age," said Seseley, uneasy at so much questioning, for she did not wish to be forced to tell an untruth. "But it is possible he is much older," she added, beginning to get confused.

"Well, well; I am sorry he did not pay my castle a visit," declared the baron. "He is very small and slight to be traveling this dangerous country alone, and I might have advised him as to his welfare."

Seseley thought that Prince Marvel would need no advice from any one as to his conduct; but she wisely refrained from speaking this thought, and the old baron walked away to glance through a slit in the stone wall at the figure of the now distant knight.

Prince Marvel was riding swiftly toward the brow of the hill, and shortly his great war-horse mounted the ascent and disappeared on its farther slope.

The youth's heart was merry and light, and he reflected joyously, as he rode along, that a whole year of freedom and fascinating adventure lay before him.

The valley in which he now found himself was very beautiful, the soft grass beneath his horse's feet being sprinkled with bright flowers, while clumps of trees stood here and there to break the monotony of the landscape.

For an hour the prince rode along, rejoicing in the free motion of his horse and breathing in the perfume-laden air. Then he found he had crossed the valley and was approaching a series of hills. These were broken by huge rocks, the ground being cluttered with boulders of rough stone. His horse speedily found a pathway leading through these rocks, but was obliged to proceed at a walk, turning first one way and then another as the path zigzagged up the hill.

Presently, being engaged in deep thought and little noting the way, Prince Marvel rode between two high walls of rock standing so close together that horse and rider could scarcely pass between the sides. Having traversed this narrow space some distance the wall opened suddenly upon a level plat of ground, where grass and trees grew. It was not a very big place, but was surely the end of the path, as all around it stood bare walls so high and steep that neither horse nor man could climb them. In the side of the rocky wall facing the entrance the traveler noticed a hollow, like the mouth of a cave, across which was placed an iron gate. And above the gateway was painted in red letters on the gray stone the following words:

WUL-TAKIM KING OF THIEVES ------ HIS TREASURE HOUSE KEEP OUT

Prince Marvel laughed on reading this, and after getting down from his saddle he advanced to the iron gate and peered through its heavy bars.

"I have no idea who this Wul-Takim is," he said, "for I know nothing at all of the ways of men outside the forest in which I have always dwelt. But thieves are bad people, I am quite sure, and since Wul-Takim is the king of thieves he must be by far the worst man on this island."

Then he saw, through the bars of the gate, that a great cavern lay beyond, in which were stacked treasures of all sorts: rich cloths, golden dishes and ornaments, gemmed coronets and bracelets, cleverly forged armor, shields and battle-axes. Also there were casks and bales of merchandise of every sort.

The gate appeared to have no lock, so Prince Marvel opened it and walked in. Then he perceived, perched on the very top of a pyramid of casks, the form of a boy, who sat very still and watched him with a look of astonishment upon his face.

"What are you doing up there?" asked the prince.

"Nothing," said the boy. "If I moved the least little bit this pile of casks would topple over, and I should be thrown to the ground."

"Well," returned the prince, "what of it?"

But just then he glanced at the ground and saw why the boy did not care to tumble down. For in the earth were planted many swords, with their sharp blades pointing upward, and to fall upon these meant serious wounds and perhaps death.

"Oh, ho!" cried Marvel; "I begin to understand. You are a prisoner."

"Yes; as you will also be shortly," answered the boy. "And then you will understand another thing, that you were very reckless ever to enter this cave."

"Why?" inquired the prince, who really knew little of the world, and was interested in everything he saw and heard.

"Because it is the stronghold of the robber king, and when you opened that gate you caused a bell to ring far down on the hillside. So the robbers are now warned that an enemy is in their cave, and they will soon arrive to make you a prisoner, even as I am."

"Ah, I see!" said the prince, with a laugh, "It is a rather clever contrivance; but having been warned in time I should indeed be foolish to be caught in such a trap."

With this he half drew his sword, but thinking that robbers were not worthy to be slain with its untarnished steel, he pushed it back into the jeweled scabbard and looked around for another weapon. A stout oaken staff lay upon the ground, and this he caught up and ran with it from the cave, placing himself just beside the narrow opening that led into this rock-encompassed plain. For he quickly saw that this was the only way any one could enter or leave the place, and therefore knew the robbers were coming up the narrow gorge even as he had himself done.

Soon they were heard stumbling along at a rapid pace, crying to one another to make haste and catch the intruder. The first that came through the opening received so sharp a blow upon the head from Prince Marvel's oak staff that he fell to the ground and lay still, while the next was treated in a like manner and fell beside his comrade.

Perhaps the thieves had not expected so sturdy an enemy, for they continued to rush through the opening in the rocks and to fall beneath the steady blows of the prince's staff until every one of them lay senseless before the victor. At first they had piled themselves upon one another very neatly; but the pile got so high at last that the prince was obliged to assist the last thieves to leap to the top of the heap before they completely lost their senses.

I have no doubt our prince, feeling himself yet strange in the new form he had acquired, and freshly transported from the forest glades in which he had always lived, was fully as much astonished at his deed of valor as were the robbers themselves; and if he shuddered a little when looking upon the heap of senseless thieves you must forgive him this weakness. For he straightway resolved to steel his heart to such sights and to be every bit as stern and severe as a mortal knight would have been.

Throwing down his staff he ran to the cave again, and stepping between the sword points he approached the pile of casks and held out his arms to the boy who was perched upon the top.

"The thieves are conquered," he cried. "Jump down!"

"I won't," said the boy.

"Why not?" inquired the prince.

"Can't you see I'm very miserable?" asked the boy, in return; "don't you understand that every minute I expect to fall upon those sword points?"

"But I will catch you," cried the prince.

"I don't want you to catch me," said the boy. "I want to be miserable. It's the first chance I've ever had, and I'm enjoying my misery very much."

This speech so astonished Prince Marvel that for a moment he stood motionless. Then he retorted, angrily:

"You're a fool!"

"If I wasn't so miserable up here, I'd come down and thrash you for that," said the boy, with a sigh.

This answer so greatly annoyed Prince Marvel that he gave the central cask of the pyramid a sudden push, and the next moment the casks were tumbling in every direction, while the boy fell headlong in their midst.

But Marvel caught him deftly in his arms, and so saved him from the sword points.

"There!" he said, standing the boy upon his feet; "now you are released from your misery."

"And I should be glad to punish you for your interference," declared the boy, gloomily eying his preserver, "had you not saved my life by catching me. According to the code of honor of knighthood I can not harm one who has saved my life until I have returned the obligation. Therefore, for the present I shall pardon your insulting speeches and actions."

"But you have also saved my life," answered Prince Marvel; "for had you not warned me of the robbers' return they would surely have caught me."

"True," said the boy, brightening up; "therefore our score is now even. But take care not to affront me again, for hereafter I will show you no mercy!"

Prince Marvel looked at the boy with wonder. He was about his own size, yet strong and well formed, and he would have been handsome except for the expression of discontent upon his face. Yet his manner and words were so absurd and unnatural that the prince was more amused than angered by his new acquaintance, and presently laughed in his face.

"If all the people in this island are like you," he said, "I shall have lots of fun with them. And you are only a boy, after all."

"I'm bigger than you!" declared the other, glaring fiercely at the prince.

"How much bigger?" asked Marvel, his eyes twinkling.

"Oh, ever so much!"

"Then fetch along that coil of rope, and follow me," said Prince Marvel.

"Fetch the rope yourself!" retorted the boy, bluntly. "I'm not your servant." Then he put his hands in his pockets and coolly walked out of the cave to look at the pile of senseless robbers.

Prince Marvel made no reply, but taking the coil of rope on his shoulder he carried it to where the thieves lay and threw it down beside them. Then he cut lengths from the coil with his sword and bound the limbs of each robber securely. Within a half-hour he had laid out a row of thieves extending half way across the grassy plain, and on counting their number he found he had captured fifty-nine of them.

This task being accomplished and the robbers rendered helpless, Prince Marvel turned to the boy who stood watching him.

"Get a suit of armor from the cave, and a strong sword, and then return here," he said, in a stern voice.

"Why should I do that?" asked the boy, rather impudently.

"Because I am going to fight you for disobeying my orders; and if you do not protect yourself I shall probably kill you."

"That sounds pleasant," said the boy. "But if you should prove my superior in skill I beg you will not kill me at once, but let me die a lingering death."

"Why?" asked the prince.

"Because I shall suffer more, and that will be delightful."

"I am not anxious to kill you, nor to make you suffer," said Marvel, "all that I ask is that you acknowledge me your master."

"I won't!" answered the boy. "I acknowledge no master in all the world!"

"Then you must fight," declared the prince, gravely. "If you win, I will promise to serve you faithfully; and if I conquer you, then you must acknowledge me your master, and obey my commands."

"Agreed!" cried the boy, with sudden energy, and he rushed into the cave and soon returned clad in armor and bearing a sword and shield. On the shield was pictured a bolt of lightning.

"Lightning will soon strike those three girls whose champion you seem to be," he said tauntingly.

"The three girls defy your lightning!" returned the prince with a smile. "I see you are brave enough."

"Brave! Why should I not be?" answered the boy proudly. "I am the Lord Nerle, the son of Neggar, the chief baron of Heg!"

The other bowed low.

"I am pleased to know your station," he said. "I am called Prince Marvel, and this is my first adventure."

"And likely to be your last," exclaimed the boy, sneeringly. "For I am stronger than you, and I have fought many times with full grown men."

"Are you ready?" asked Prince Marvel, for answer.

"Yes."

Then the swords clashed and sparks flew from the blades. But it was not for long. Suddenly Nerle's sword went flying through the air and shattered its blade against a wall of rock. He scowled at Prince Marvel a moment, who smiled back at him. Then the boy rushed into the cave and returned with another sword.

Scarcely had the weapons crossed again when with a sudden blow Prince Marvel snapped Nerle's blade in two, and followed this up with a sharp slap upon his ear with the flat of his own sword that fairly bewildered the boy, and made him sit down on the grass to think what had happened to him.

Then Prince Marvel's merry laugh rang far across the hills, and so delighted was he at the astonished expression upon Nerle's face that it was many minutes before he could control his merriment and ask his foeman if he had had enough fight.

"I suppose I have," replied the boy, rubbing his ear tenderly. "That blow stings most deliciously. But it is a hard thought that the son of Baron Neggar should serve Prince Marvel!"

"Do not worry about that," said the prince; "for I assure you my rank is so far above your own that it is no degradation for the son of Neggar to serve me. But come, we must dispose of these thieves. What is the proper fate for such men?"

"They are always hanged," answered Nerle, getting upon his feet.

"Well, there are trees handy," remarked the prince, although his girlish heart insisted on making him shiver in spite of his resolve to be manly and stern. "Let us get to work and hang them as soon as possible. And then we can proceed upon our journey."

Nerle now willingly lent his assistance to his new master, and soon they had placed a rope around the neck of each thief and were ready to dangle them all from the limbs of the trees.

But at this juncture the thieves began to regain consciousness, and now Wul-Takim, the big, red-bearded king of the thieves, sat up and asked:

"Who is our conqueror?"

"Prince Marvel," answered Nerle.

"And what army assisted him?" inquired Wul-Takim, curiously gazing upon the prince.

"He conquered you alone and single-handed," said Nerle.

Hearing this, the big king began to weep bitterly, and the tear-drops ran down his face in such a stream that Prince Marvel ordered Nerle to wipe them away with his handkerchief, as the thief's hands were tied behind his back.

"To think!" sobbed Wul-Takim, miserably; "only to think, that after all my terrible deeds and untold wickedness, I have been captured by a mere boy! Oh, boo-hoo! boo-hoo! boo-hoo! It is a terrible disgrace!"

"You will not have to bear it long," said the prince, soothingly. "I am going to hang you in a few minutes."

"Thanks! Thank you very much!" answered the king, ceasing to weep. "I have always expected to be hanged some day, and I am glad no one but you two boys will witness me when my feet begin kicking about."

"I shall not kick," declared another of the thieves, who had also regained his senses. "I shall sing while I am being hanged."

"But you can not, my good Gunder," protested the king; "for the rope will cut off your breath, and no man can sing without breath."

"Then I shall whistle," said Gunder, composedly.

The king cast at him a look of reproach, and turning to Prince Marvel he said:

"It will be a great task to string up so many thieves. You look tired. Permit me to assist you to hang the others, and then I will climb into a tree and hang myself from a strong branch, with as little bother as possible."

"Oh, I won't think of troubling you," exclaimed Marvel, with a laugh. "Having conquered you alone, I feel it my duty to hang you without Assistance, save that of my esquire."

"It's no trouble, I assure you; but suit your own convenience," said the thief, carelessly. Then he cast his eye toward the cave and asked: "What will you do with all our treasure?"

"Give it to the poor," said Prince Marvel, promptly.

"What poor?"

"Oh, the poorest people I can find."

"Will you permit me to advise you in this matter?" asked the king of thieves, politely.

"Yes, indeed; for I am a stranger in this land," returned the prince.

"Well, I know a lot of people who are so poor that they have no possessions whatever, neither food to eat, houses to live in, nor any clothing but that which covers their bodies. They can call no man friend, nor will any lift a hand to help them. Indeed, good sir, I verily believe they will soon perish miserably unless you come to their assistance!"

"Poor creatures!" exclaimed Prince Marvel, with ready sympathy; "tell me who they are, and I will divide amongst them all your ill-gotten gains."

"They are ourselves," replied the king of thieves, with a sigh.

Marvel looked at him in amazement, and then burst into joyous laughter.

"Yourselves!" he cried, greatly amused.

"Indeed, yes!" said Wul-Takim, sadly. "There are no poorer people in all the world, for we have ropes about our necks and are soon to be hanged. To-morrow we shall not have even our flesh left, for the crows will pick our bones."

"That is true," remarked Marvel, thoughtfully. "But, if I restore to you the treasure, how will it benefit you, since you are about to die?"

"Must you really hang us?" asked the thief.

"Yes; I have decreed it, and you deserve your fate."

"Why?"

"Because you have wickedly taken from helpless people their property, and committed many other crimes besides."

"But I have reformed! We have all reformed have we not, brothers?"

"We have!" answered the other thieves, who, having regained their senses, were listening to this conversation with much interest.

"And, if you will return to us our treasure, we will promise never to steal again, but to remain honest men and enjoy our wealth in peace," promised the king.

"Honest men could not enjoy treasures they have stolen," said Prince Marvel.

"True; but this treasure is now yours, having been won by you in fair battle. And if you present it to us it will no longer be stolen treasure, but a generous gift from a mighty prince, which we may enjoy with clear consciences."

"Yet there remains the fact that I have promised to hang you," suggested Prince Marvel, with a smile, for the king amused him greatly.

"Not at all! Not at all!" cried Wul-Takim. "You promised to hang fifty-nine thieves, and there is no doubt the fifty-nine thieves deserved to be hung. But, consider! We have all reformed our ways and become honest men; so it would be a sad and unkindly act to hang fifty-nine honest men!"

"What think you, Nerle?" asked the Prince, turning to his esquire.

"Why, the rogue seems to speak truth," said Nerle, scratching his head with a puzzled air, "yet, if he speaks truth, there is little difference between a rogue and an honest man. Ask him, my master, what caused them all to reform so suddenly."

"Because we were about to die, and we thought it a good way to save our lives," replied the robber king.

"That's an honest answer, anyway," said Nerle. "Perhaps, sir, they have really reformed."

"And if so, I will not have the death of fifty-nine honest men on my conscience," declared the prince. Then he turned to Wul-Takim and added: "I will release you and give you the treasure, as you request. But you owe me allegiance from this time forth, and if I ever hear of your becoming thieves again, I promise to return and hang every one of you."

"Never fear!" answered Wul-Takim, joyfully. "It is hard work to steal, and while we have so much treasure it is wholly unnecessary. Moreover, having accepted from you our lives and our fortunes, we shall hereafter be your devoted servants, and whenever you need our services you have but to call upon us, and we will support you loyally and gladly."

"I accept your service," answered the prince, graciously.

And then he unbound the fifty-nine honest men and took the ropes from their necks. As nightfall was fast approaching the new servants set to work to prepare a great feast in honor of their master. It was laid in the middle of the grassy clearing, that all might sit around and celebrate the joyous occasion.

"Do you think you can trust these men?" asked Nerle, suspiciously.

"Why not?" replied the prince. "They have been exceedingly wicked, it is true; but they are now intent upon being exceedingly good. Let us encourage them in this. If we mistrusted all who have ever done an evil act there would be fewer honest people in the world. And if it were as interesting to do a good act as an evil one there is no doubt every one would choose the good."

Chapter 6 - The Troubles of Nerle

That night Prince Marvel slept within the cave, surrounded by the fifty-nine reformed thieves, and suffered no harm at their hands. In the morning, accompanied by his esquire, Nerle, who was mounted upon a spirited horse brought him by Wul-Takim, he charged the honest men to remember their promises, bade them good by, and set out in search of further adventure.

As they left the clearing by the narrow passage that led between the overhanging rocks, the prince looked back and saw that the sign above the gate of the cave, which had told of the thieves' treasure house, had been changed. It now read as follows:

WUL-TAKIM KING OF HONEST MEN ------- HIS PLEASURE HOUSE WALK IN

"That is much better," laughed the prince. "I accomplished some good by my adventure, anyway!"

Nerle did not reply. He seemed especially quiet and thoughtful as he rode by his master's side, and after they had traveled some distance in silence Prince Marvel said:

"Tell me how you came to be in the cave of thieves, and perched upon the casks where I found you."

"It is a sad story," returned Nerle, with a sigh; "but since you request me to tell it, the tale may serve to relieve the tedium of your journey.

"My father is a mighty baron, very wealthy and with a heart so kind that he has ever taken pleasure in thrusting on me whatever gift he could think of. I had not a single desire unsatisfied, for before I could wish for anything it was given me.

"My mother was much like my father. She and her women were always making jams, jellies, candies, cakes and the like for me to eat; so I never knew the pleasure of hunger. My clothes were the gayest satins and velvets, richly made and sewn with gold and silver braid; so it was impossible to wish for more in the way of apparel. They let me study my lessons whenever I felt like it and go fishing or hunting as I pleased; so I could not complain that I was unable to do just as I wanted to. All the servants obeyed my slightest wish: if I wanted to sit up late at night no one objected; if I wished to lie in bed till noon they kept the house quiet so as not to disturb me.

"This condition of affairs, as you may imagine, grew more and more tedious and exasperating the older I became. Try as I might, I could find nothing to complain of. I once saw the son of one of our servants receive a flogging; and my heart grew light. I immediately begged my father to flog me, by way of variety; and he, who could refuse me nothing, at once consented. For this reason there was less satisfaction in the operation than I had expected, although for the time being it was a distinct novelty.

"Now, no one could expect a high-spirited boy to put up with such a life as mine. With nothing to desire and no chance of doing anything that would annoy my parents, my days were dreary indeed."

He paused to wipe the tears from his eyes, and the prince murmured, sympathetically: "Poor boy! Poor boy!"

"Ah, you may well say that!" continued Nerle. "But one day a stranger came to my father's castle with tales of many troubles he had met with. He had been lost in a forest and nearly starved to death. He had been robbed and beaten and left wounded and sore by the wayside. He had begged from door to door and been refused food or assistance. In short, his story was so delightful that it made me envy him, and I yearned to suffer as he had done. When I could speak with him alone I said: 'Pray tell me how I can manage to acquire the misfortunes you have undergone. Here I have everything that I desire, and it makes me very unhappy.'

"The stranger laughed at me, at first; and I found some pleasure in the humiliation I then felt. But it did not last long, for presently he grew sober and advised me to run away from home and seek adventure.

"'Once away from your father's castle,' said he, 'troubles will fall upon you thick enough to satisfy even your longings.'

"'That is what I am afraid of!' I answered. 'I don't want to be satisfied, even with troubles. What I seek is unsatisfied longings.'

"'Nevertheless,' said he, 'I advise you to travel. Everything will probably go wrong with you, and then you will be happy.'

"I acted upon the stranger's advice and ran away from home the next day. After journeying a long time I commenced to feel the pangs of hunger, and was just beginning to enjoy myself when a knight rode by and gave me a supply of food. At this rebuff I could not restrain my tears, but while I wept my horse stumbled and threw me over his head. I hoped at first I had broken my neck, and was just congratulating myself upon the misfortune, when a witch-woman came along and rubbed some ointment upon my bruises, in spite of my protests. To my great grief the pain left me, and I was soon well again. But, as a slight compensation for my disappointment, my horse had run away; so I began my journey anew and on foot.

"That afternoon I stepped into a nest of wasps, but the thoughtless creatures flew away without stinging me. Then I met a fierce tiger, and my heart grew light and gay. 'Surely this will cause me suffering!' I cried, and advanced swiftly upon the brute. But the cowardly tiger turned tail and ran to hide in the bushes, leaving me unhurt!

"Of course, my many disappointments were some consolation; but not much. That night I slept on the bare ground, and hoped I should catch a severe cold; but no such joy was to be mine.

"Yet the next afternoon I experienced my first pleasure. The thieves caught me, stripped off all my fine clothes and jewels and beat me well. Then they carried me to their cave, dressed me in rags, and perched me on the top of the casks, where the slightest movement on my part would send me tumbling among the sword points. This was really delightful, and I was quite happy until you came and released me.

"I thought then that I might gain some pleasure by provoking you to anger; and our fight was the result. That blow on the ear was exquisite, and by forcing me to become your servant you have made me, for the first time in my life, almost contented. For I hope in your company to experience a great many griefs and disappointments."

As Nerle concluded his story Prince Marvel turned to him and grasped his hand.

"Accept my sympathy!" said he. "I know exactly how you feel, for my own life during the past few centuries has not been much different."

"The past few centuries!" gasped Nerle. "What do you mean?"

At this the prince blushed, seeing he had nearly disclosed his secret. But he said, quickly:

"Does it not seem centuries when one is unhappy?"

"It does, indeed!" responded Nerle, earnestly. "But please tell me your story."

"Not now," said Prince Marvel, with a smile. "It will please you to desire in vain to hear a tale I will not tell. Yet I promise that on the day we part company I shall inform you who I am."

Chapter 7 - The Gray Men

The adventurers gave no heed to the path they followed after leaving the cave of the reformed thieves, but their horses accidentally took the direction of the foot-hills that led into the wild interior Kingdom of Spor. Therefore the travelers, when they had finished their conversation and begun to look about them, found themselves in a rugged, mountainous country that was wholly unlike the green plains of Heg they had left behind.

Now, as I have before said, the most curious and fearful of the island people dwelt in this Kingdom of Spor. They held no friendly communication with their neighbors, and only left their own mountains to plunder and rob; and so sullen and fierce were they on these occasions that every one took good care to keep out of their way until they had gone back home again.

There was much gossip about the unknown king of Spor, who had never yet been seen by any one except his subjects; and some thought he must be one of the huge giants of Spor; and others claimed he was a dwarf, like his tiny but ferocious dart-slingers; and still others imagined him one of the barbarian tribe, or a fellow to the terrible Gray Men. But, of course, no one knew positively, and all these guesses were very wide of the mark. The only certainty about this king was that his giants, dwarfs, barbarians and Gray Men meekly acknowledged his rule and obeyed his slightest wish; for though they might be terrible to others, their king was still more terrible to them.

Into this Kingdom of Spor Prince Marvel and Nerle had now penetrated and, neither knowing nor caring where they were, continued along the faintly defined paths the horses had found. Presently, however, they were startled by a peal of shrill, elfish laughter, and raising their eyes they beheld a horrid-looking old man seated upon a high rock near by.

"Why do you laugh?" asked Prince Marvel, stopping his horse.

"Have you been invited? Tell me, have you been invited?" demanded the old man, chuckling to himself as if much amused.

"Invited where?" inquired the prince.

"To Spor, stupid! To the Kingdom of Spor! To the land of King Terribus!" shrieked the old man, going into violent peals of laughter.

"We go and come as we please," answered Prince Marvel, calmly.

"Go, yes! Go if you will. But you'll never come back, never! never! never!" The little old man seemed to consider this such a good joke that he bent nearly double with laughing, and so lost his balance and toppled off the rock, disappearing from their view; but they could hear him laugh long after they had passed on and left him far behind them.

"A strange creature!" exclaimed the prince thoughtfully.

"But perhaps he speaks truth," answered Nerle, "if, in fact, we have been rash enough to enter the Kingdom of Spor. Even my father, the bravest baron in Heg, has never dared venture within the borders of Spor. For all men fear its mysterious king."

"In that case," replied Prince Marvel, "it is time some one investigated this strange kingdom. People have left King Terribus and his wild subjects too much to themselves; instead of stirring them up and making them behave themselves."

Nerle smiled at this speech.

"They are the fiercest people on the Enchanted Island," said he, "and there are thousands upon thousands who obey this unknown king. But if you think we dare defy them I am willing to go on. Perhaps our boldness will lead them into torturing me, or starving me to death; and at the very least I ought to find much trouble and privation in the Kingdom of Spor."

"Time will determine that," said the prince, cheerfully.

They had now ridden into a narrow defile of the mountains, the pathway being lined with great fragments of rock. Happening to look over his shoulder Prince Marvel saw that as they passed these rocks a man stepped from behind each fragment and followed after them, their numbers thus constantly increasing until hundreds were silently treading in the wake of the travelers.

These men were very peculiar in appearance, their skins being as gray as the rocks themselves, while their only clothing consisted of gray cloth tunics belted around the waists with bands of gray fox-hide. They bore no weapons except that each was armed with a fork, having three sharp tines six inches in length, which the Gray Men carried stuck through their fox-hide belts.

Nerle also looked back and saw the silent throng following them, and the sight sent such a cold shiver creeping up his spine that he smiled with pleasure. There was no way to avoid the Gray Men, for the path was so narrow that the horsemen could not turn aside; but Prince Marvel was not disturbed, and seemed not to mind being followed, so long as no one hindered his advance.

He rode steadily on, Nerle following, and after climbing upward for a long way the path began to descend, presently leading them into a valley of wide extent, in the center of which stood an immense castle with tall domes that glittered as if covered with pure gold. A broad roadway paved with white marble reached from the mountain pass to the entrance of this castle, and on each side of this roadway stood lines of monstrous giants, armed with huge axes thrust into their belts and thick oak clubs, studded with silver spikes, which were carried over their left shoulders.

The assembled giants were as silent as the Gray Men, and stood motionless while Prince Marvel and Nerle rode slowly up the marble roadway. But all their brows were scowling terribly and their eyes were red and glaring, as if they were balls of fire.

"I begin to feel very pleasant," said Nerle, "for surely we shall not get away from these folks without a vast deal of trouble. They do not seem to oppose our advance, but it is plain they will not allow us any chance of retreat."

"We do not wish to retreat," declared the prince.

Nerle cast another glance behind, and saw that the Gray Men had halted at the edge of the valley, while the giants were closing up as soon as the horses passed them and now marched in close file in their rear.

"It strikes me," he muttered, softly, "that this is like to prove our last adventure." But although Prince Marvel might have heard the words he made no reply, being evidently engaged in deep thought.

As they drew nearer the castle it towered above them like a veritable mountain, so big and high was it; and the walls cast deep shadows far around, as if twilight had fallen. They heard the loud blare of a trumpet sounding far up on the battlements; the portals of the castle suddenly opened wide, and they entered a vast courtyard paved with plates of gold. Tiny dwarfs, so crooked that they resembled crabs, rushed forward and seized the bridles of the horses, while the strangers slowly dismounted and looked around them.

While the steeds were being led to the stables an old man, clothed in a flowing robe as white in color as his beard, bowed before Prince Marvel and said in a soft voice:

"Follow me!"

The prince stretched his arms, yawned as if tired with his ride, and then glared upon the old man with an expression of haughty surprise.

"I follow no one!" said he, proudly. "I am Prince Marvel, sirrah, and if the owner of this castle wishes to see me I shall receive him here, as befits my rank and station."

The man looked surprised, but only bowed lower than before.

"It is the king's command," he answered.

"The king?"

"Yes; you are in the castle of King Terribus, the lord and ruler of Spor."

"That is different," remarked the prince, lightly. "Still, I will follow no man. Point out the way and I will go to meet his Majesty."

The old man extended a lean and trembling finger toward an archway. Prince Marvel strode forward, followed by Nerle, and passing under the arch he threw open a door at the far end and boldly entered the throne-room of King Terribus.

Chapter 8 - The Fool-Killer

The room was round, with a dome at the top. The bare walls were of gray stone, with square, open windows set full twenty feet from the floor. Rough gray stone also composed the floor, and in the center of the room stood one great rock with a seat hollowed in its middle. This was the throne, and round about it stood a swarm of men and women dressed in rich satins, velvets and brocades, brilliantly ornamented with gold and precious stones. The men were of many shapes and sizes, giants and dwarfs being among them. The women all seemed young and beautiful.

Prince Marvel cast but a passing glance at this assemblage, for his eye quickly sought the rude throne on which was seated King Terribus.

The personal appearance of this monster was doubtless the most hideous known in that age of the world. His head was large and shaped like an egg; it was bright scarlet in color and no hair whatever grew upon it. It had three eyes; one in the center of his face, one on the top of his head and one in the back. Thus he was always able to see in every direction at the same time. His nose was shaped like an elephant's trunk, and swayed constantly from side to side. His mouth was very wide and had no lips at all, two rows of sharp and white teeth being always plainly visible beneath the swaying nose.

King Terribus, although surrounded by so splendid a court, wore a simple robe of gray cloth, with no ornament or other finery, and his strange and fearful appearance was strongly contrasted with the glittering raiment of his courtiers and the beauty of his ladies in waiting.

When Prince Marvel, with Nerle marching close behind, entered the great room, Terribus looked at him sharply a moment, and then bowed. And when he bowed the eye upon the top of his head also looked sharply at the intruders.

Then the king spoke, his voice sounding so sweet and agreeable that it almost shocked Nerle, who had expected to hear a roar like that from a wild beast.

"Why are you here?" asked Terribus.

"Partly by chance and partly from curiosity," answered Prince Marvel. "No one in this island, except your own people, had ever seen the king of Spor; so, finding myself in your country, I decided to come here and have a look at you."

The faces of the people who stood about the throne wore frightened looks at the unheard of boldness of this speech to their terrible monarch. But the king merely nodded and inquired:

"Since you have seen me, what do you think of me?"

"I am sorry you asked that question," returned the prince; "for I must confess you are a very frightful-looking creature, and not at all agreeable to gaze upon."

"Ha! you are honest, as well as frank," exclaimed the king. "But that is the reason I do not leave my kingdom, as you will readily understand. And that is the reason I never permit strangers to come here, under penalty of death. So long as no one knows the King of Spor is a monster people will not gossip about my looks, and I am very sensitive regarding my personal appearance. You will perhaps understand that if I could have chosen I should have been born beautiful instead of ugly."

"I certainly understand that. And permit me to say I wish you were beautiful. I shall probably dream of you for many nights," added the prince.

"Not for many," said King Terribus, quietly. "By coming here you have chosen death, and the dead do not dream."

"Why should I die?" inquired Prince Marvel, curiously.

"Because you have seen me. Should I allow you to go away you would tell the world about my ugly face. I do not like to kill you, believe me; but you must pay the penalty of your rashness, you and the man behind you."

Nerle smiled at this; but whether from pride at being called a man or in pleasurable anticipation of the sufferings to come I leave you to guess.

"Will you allow me to object to being killed?" asked the prince.

"Certainly," answered the king, courteously. "I expect you to object. It is natural. But it will do you no good."

Then Terribus turned to an attendant and commanded:

"Send hither the Fool-Killer."

At this Prince Marvel laughed outright.

"The Fool-Killer!" he cried; "surely your Majesty does me little credit. Am I, then, a fool?"

"You entered my kingdom uninvited," retorted the king, "and you tell me to my face I am ugly. Moreover, you laugh when I condemn you to death. From this I conclude the Fool-Killer is the proper one to execute you. Behold!"

Marvel turned quickly, to find a tall, stalwart man standing behind him. His features were strong but very grave, and the prince caught a look of compassion in his eye as their gaze met. His skin was fair and without blemish, a robe of silver cloth fell from his shoulders, and in his right hand he bore a gleaming sword.

"Well met!" cried Marvel, heartily, as he bowed to the Fool-Killer. "I have often heard your name mentioned, but 'tis said in the world that you are a laggard in your duty."

"Had I my way," answered the Fool-Killer, "my blade would always drip. It is my master, yonder, who thwarts my duty." And he nodded toward King Terribus.

"Then you should exercise your right on him, and cleave the ugly head from his shoulders," declared the prince.

"Nay, unless I interfered with the Fool-Killer," said the king, "I should soon have no subjects left to rule; for at one time or another they all deserve the blade."

"Why, that may be true enough," replied Prince Marvel. "But I think, under such circumstances, your Fool-Killer is a needless servant. So I will rid you of him in a few moments."

With that he whipped out his sword and stood calmly confronting the Fool-Killer, whose grave face never changed in expression as he advanced menacingly upon his intended victim. The blades clashed together, and that of the Fool-Killer broke short off at the hilt. He took a step backward, stumbled and fell prone upon the rocky floor, while Prince Marvel sprang forward and pressed the point of his sword against his opponent's breast.

"Hold!" cried the king, starting to his feet. "Would you slay my Fool-Killer? Think of the harm you would do the world!"

"But he is laggard and unfaithful to his calling!" answered the prince, sternly.

"Nevertheless, if he remove but one fool a year he is a benefit to mankind," declared the king. "Release him, I pray you!"

Then the victor withdrew his sword and stood aside, while the Fool-Killer slowly got upon his feet and bowed humbly before the king.

"Go!" shouted Terribus, his eye flashing angrily. "You have humiliated me before my enemy. As an atonement see that you kill me a fool a day for sixty days."

Hearing this command, many of the people about the throne began to tremble; but the king paid no attention to their fears, and the Fool-Killer bowed again before his master and withdrew from the chamber.

Chapter 9 - The Royal Dragon of Spor

"Now," said Terribus, regarding the prince gloomily, "I must dispose of you in another way."

For a moment he dropped his scarlet head in thought. Then he turned fiercely upon his attendants.

"Let the Wrestler come forward!" he shouted, as loudly as his mild voice would carry.

Instantly a tall blackamoor advanced from the throng and cast off his flowing robe, showing a strong figure clad only in a silver loincloth.

"Crack me this fellow's bones!" commanded Terribus.

"I beg your Majesty will not compel me to touch him," said Prince Marvel, with a slight shudder; "for his skin is greasy, and will soil my hands. Here, Nerle!" he continued, turning to his esquire, "dispose of this black man, and save me the trouble."

Nerle laughed pleasantly. The black was a powerfully built man, and compared with Nerle and the prince, who had but the stature of boys, he towered like a very giant in size. Nevertheless, Nerle did not hesitate to spring upon the Wrestler, who with a quick movement sent the boy crashing against the stone pavement.

Nerle was much bruised by the fall, and as he painfully raised himself to his feet a great lump was swelling behind his left ear, where his head had struck the floor, and he was so dizzy that the room seemed swimming around him in a circle. But he gave a happy little laugh, and said to the prince, gratefully:

"Thank you very much, my master! The fall is hurting me delightfully. I almost feel as if I could cry, and that would be joy indeed!"

"Well," answered the prince, with a sigh, "I see I must get my hands greased after all" for the black's body had really been greased to enable him to elude the grasp of his opponents.

But Marvel made a quick leap and seized the Wrestler firmly around the waist. The next moment, to the astonishment of all, the black man flew swiftly into the air, plunged through one of the open windows high up in the wall, and disappeared from view. When the king and his people again turned their wondering eyes upon the prince he was wiping his hands carefully upon a silk handkerchief.

At this sight a pretty young girl, who stood near the throne, laughed aloud, and the sound of her laughter made King Terribus very angry.

"Come here!" he commanded, sternly. The girl stepped forward, her face now pale and frightened, while tear-drops trembled upon the lashes that fringed her downcast eyes. "You have dared to laugh at the humiliation of your king," said Terribus, his horrid face more crimson than ever, "and as atonement I command that you drink of the poisoned cup."

Instantly a dwarf came near, bearing a beautiful golden goblet in his crooked hands.

"Drink!" he said, an evil leer upon his face.

The girl well knew this goblet contained a vile poison, one drop of which on her tongue would cause death; so she hesitated, trembling and shrinking from the ordeal.

Prince Marvel looked into her sweet face with pitying eyes, and stepping quickly to her side, took her hand in his.

"Now drink!" he said, smiling upon her; "the poison will not hurt you."

She drank obediently, while the dwarf chuckled with awful glee and the king looked on eagerly, expecting her to fall dead at his feet. But instead the girl stood upright and pressed Marvel's hand, looking gratefully into his face.

"You are a fairy!" she whispered, so low that no one else heard her voice. "I knew that you would save me."

"Keep my secret," whispered the prince in return, and still holding her hand he led her back to her former place.

King Terribus was almost wild with rage and disappointment, and his elephant nose twisted and squirmed horribly.

"So you dare to thwart my commands, do you!" he cried, excitedly. "Well, we shall soon see which of us is the more powerful. I have decreed your death and die you shall!"

For a moment his eye roved around the chamber uncertainly. Then he shouted, suddenly:

"Ho, there! Keepers of the royal menagerie, appear!"

Three men entered the room and bowed before the king. They were of the Gray Men of the mountains, who had followed Prince Marvel and Nerle through the rocky passes.

"Bring hither the Royal Dragon," cried the king, "and let him consume these strangers before my very eyes!"

The men withdrew, and presently was heard a distant shouting, followed by a low rumbling sound, with groans, snorts, roars and a hissing like steam from the spout of a teakettle.

The noise and shouting drew nearer, while the people huddled together like frightened sheep; and then suddenly the doors flew open and the Royal Dragon advanced to the center of the room.

This creature was at once the pride and terror of the Kingdom of Spor. It was more than thirty feet in length and covered everywhere with large green scales set with diamonds, making the dragon, when it moved, a very glittering spectacle. Its eyes were as big as pie-plates, and its mouth, when wide opened, fully as large as a bath-tub. Its tail was very long and ended in a golden ball, such as you see on the top of flagstaffs. Its legs, which were as thick as those of an elephant, had scales which were set with rubies and emeralds. It had two monstrous, big ears and two horns of carved ivory, and its teeth were also carved into various fantastic shapes; such as castles, horses' heads, chinamen and griffins, so that if any of them broke it would make an excellent umbrella handle.

The Royal Dragon of Spor came crawling into the throne-room rather clumsily, groaning and moaning with every step and waving its ears like two blankets flying from a clothesline.

The king looked on it and frowned.

"Why are you not breathing fire and brimstone?" he demanded, angrily.

"Why, I was caught out in a gale the other night," returned the Dragon, rubbing the back of its ear with its left front paw, as it paused and looked at the king, "and the wind put out my fire."

"Then why didn't you light it again?" asked Terribus, turning on the keepers.

"We, we were out of matches, your Majesty!" stammered the trembling Gray Men.

"So, ho!" yelled the king, and was about to order the keepers beheaded; but just then Nerle pulled out his match-box, lit one of the matches, and held it in front of the Dragon's mouth. Instantly the creature's breath caught fire; and it began to breathe flames a yard in length.

"That's better," sighed the Dragon, contentedly. "I hope your Majesty is now satisfied."

"No, I am not satisfied!" declared King Terribus. "Why do you not lash your tail?"

"Ah, I can't do that!" replied the Dragon. "It's all stiffened up with rheumatism from the dampness of my cave. It hurts too much to lash it."

"Well, then, gnash your teeth!" commanded the king.

"Tut, tut!" answered the Dragon, mildly; "I can't do that, either; for since you had them so beautifully carved it makes my teeth ache to gnash them."

"Well, then, what are you good for?" cried the king, in a fury.

"Don't I look awful? Am I not terrible to gaze on?" inquired the Dragon, proudly, as it breathed out red and yellow flames and made them curl in circles around its horns. "I guess there's no need for me to suggest terror to any one that happens to see me," it added, winking one of the pie-plate eyes at King Terribus.

The king looked at the monster critically, and it really seemed to him that it was a frightful thing to behold. So he curbed his anger and said, in his ordinary sweet voice:

"I have called you here to destroy these two strangers."

"How?" asked the Dragon, looking upon Prince Marvel and Nerle with interest.

"I am not particular," answered the king. "You may consume them With your fiery breath, or smash them with your tail, or grind them to atoms between your teeth, or tear them to pieces with your claws. Only, do hurry up and get it over with!"

"Hm-m-m!" said the Dragon, thoughtfully, as if it didn't relish the job; "this one isn't Saint George, is it?"

"No, no!" exclaimed the king, irritably; "it's Prince Marvel. Do get to work as soon as possible."

"Prince Marvel, Prince Marvel," repeated the Dragon. "Why, there isn't a prince in the whole world named Marvel! I'm pretty well posted on the history of royal families, you know. I'm afraid he's Saint George in disguise."

"Isn't your name Prince Marvel?" inquired the king, turning to the boyish-looking stranger.

"It is," answered Marvel.

"Well, it's mighty strange I've never heard of you," persisted the Dragon. "But tell me, please, how would you prefer to be killed?"

"Oh, I'm not going to be killed at all," replied the prince, laughing.

"Do you hear that, Terribus?" asked the Dragon, turning to the king; "he says he isn't going to be killed."

"But I say he is!" cried Terribus. "I have decreed his death."

"But do you suppose I'm going to kill a man against his will?" inquired the Dragon, in a reproachful voice; "and such a small man, too! Do you take me for a common assassin, or a murderer?"

"Do you intend to obey my orders?" roared the king.

"No, I don't; and that's flat!" returned the Dragon, sharply. "It's time for me to take my cough medicine; so if you've nothing more to say I'll go back to my cave."

"Go, go, go!" shrieked the king, stamping his foot in passion. "You've outlived your usefulness! You're a coward! You're a traitor! You're a – a – a -"

"I'm a dragon and a gentleman!" answered the monster, proudly, as the king paused for lack of a word; "and I believe I know what's proper for dragons to do and what isn't. I've learned wisdom from my father, who got into trouble with Saint George, and if I fought with this person who calls himself Prince Marvel, I'd deserve to be a victim of your Fool-Killer. Oh, I know my business, King Terribus; and if you knew yours, you'd get rid of this pretended prince as soon as possible!"

With this speech he winked at Prince Marvel, turned soberly around and crawled from the room. One of the keepers got too near and the Dragon's breath set fire to his robe, the flames being with difficulty extinguished; and the gold ball on the end of the Dragon's tail struck a giant upon his shins and made him dance and howl in pain.

But, aside from these slight accidents, the monster managed to leave the throne-room without undue confusion, and every one, including the king, seemed glad to be rid of him.

Chapter 10 - Prince Marvel Wins His Fight

When the door had closed on the Royal Dragon, King Terribus turned again to Prince Marvel, while his crimson face glowed with embarrassment, and his front eye rolled with baffled rage as he thought how vain had been all his efforts to kill this impudent invader of his domains.

But his powers were by no means exhausted. He was a mighty king, the mightiest of all in the Enchanted Island, he believed and ways to destroy his enemies were numerous.

"Send for a hundred of my Gray Men!" he suddenly cried; and a courtier ran at once to summon them. The Gray Men would obey his orders without question, he well knew. They were silent, stubborn, quick, and faithful to their king. Terribus had but to command and his will would be obeyed.

They entered the room so quietly that Nerle never knew they were there until he turned and found the hundred gray ones standing close together in the center of the hall. Then Prince Marvel came to Nerle's side and whispered something in his ear.

"Will you obey my orders?" they heard the king ask. And the Gray Men, with their eyes fixed upon their master, nodded all their hundred heads and put their hands upon the dangerous three-tined forks that were stuck in every one of the hundred belts.

Prince Marvel handed one end of a coiled rope to Nerle, and then they both sprang forward and ran around the spot where the hundred Gray Men stood huddled together. Then they were pulled closer together than before, closer, and still closer, for the prince and Nerle had surrounded them with the rope and were tying the two ends together in a tight knot. The rope cut into the waists of those on the outside, and they pressed inward against their fellows until there was scarcely space to stick a knife-blade between any two of them. When the prince had tied the rope firmly King

Terribus, who had been looking on amazed, saw that his hundred Gray Men were fastened together like a bundle of kindling-wood, and were unable to stir hand or foot.

And, while he still gazed open-mouthed at the strange sight, Prince Marvel tilted the bundle of men up on its edge and rolled it out of the door. It went rolling swiftly through the courtyard and bounded down the castle steps, where the rope broke and the men fell sprawling in all directions on the marble walk.

King Terribus sighed, for such treatment of his Gray Men, whom he dearly loved, made him very unhappy.

But more than ever was he resolved to kill these impudent strangers, who, in the very heart of his kingdom where thousands bowed to his will, dared openly defy his power. So, after a moment's thought, Terribus beckoned to a dwarf who, robed in gay and glittering apparel, stood near his throne.

"Summon the royal Dart Slingers!" he said, with a scowl.

The little man bowed and hastened away, to return presently with twenty curiously crooked dwarfs, each armed with a sling and a quiver full of slender, sharp-pointed darts.

"Slay me these strangers!" exclaimed the king, in his gruffest voice.

Now Nerle, when he beheld these terrible Dart Slingers, of whom he had heard many tales in his boyhood, began to shiver and shake with fright, so that his teeth rattled one upon another. And he reflected: "Soon shall I be content, for these darts will doubtless pierce every part of my body."

The dwarfs formed a line at one side of the gloomy throne-room, and Prince Marvel, who had been earnestly regarding them, caught Nerle by the arm and led him to the opposite wall.

"Stand close behind me and you will be safe," he whispered to his esquire.

Then each dwarf fixed a dart in his sling, and at a word from their chief they all drew back their arms and launched a shower of the sharp missiles at the strangers.

Swift and true they sped, each dart intended to pierce the body of the youthful knight who stood so calm before them. Prince Marvel had raised his right arm, and in his hand was a small leather sack, with a wide mouth. As the darts flew near him a strange thing happened: they each and all swerved from their true course and fell rattling into the leathern sack, to the wonder of the royal slingers and the dismay of King Terribus himself.

"Again!" screamed the king, his usually mild voice hoarse with anger.

So again the dwarfs cast their darts, and again the leathern sack caught them every one. Another flight followed, and yet another, till the magic sack was packed full of the darts and not a dwarf had one remaining in his quiver.

Amid the awed silence of the beholders of this feat the merry laughter of Prince Marvel rang loud and clear; for the sight of the puzzled and terrified faces about him was very comical. Plucking a dart from the sack he raised his arm and cried:

"Now it is my turn. You shall have back your darts!"

"Hold!" shouted the king, in great fear. "Do not, I beg you, slay my faithful servants." And with a wave of his hand he dismissed the dwarfs, who were glad to rush from the room and escape.

Nerle wiped the tears from his eyes, for he was sorely disappointed at having again escaped all pain and discomfort; but Prince Marvel seated himself quietly upon a stool and looked at the scowling face of King Terribus with real amusement.

The monarch of Spor had never before been so foiled and scorned by any living creature. Defeated and humbled before his own people, he bowed his crimson head on his hands and sullenly regarded his foe with his top eye. Then it was that the idea came to him that no ordinary mortal could have thwarted him so easily, and he began to fear he was dealing, perhaps unawares, with some great magician or sorcerer. That a fairy should have assumed a mortal form he never once considered, for such a thing was until then unheard of in the Enchanted Island of Yew. But with the knowledge that he had met his master, whoever he might prove to be, and that further attempts upon the stranger's life might lead to his own undoing, King Terribus decided to adopt a new line of conduct, hoping to accomplish by stratagem what he could not do by force. To be sure, there remained his regiment of Giants, the pride of his kingdom; but Terribus dreaded to meet with another defeat; and he was not at all sure, after what had happened, that the giants would succeed in conquering or destroying the strangers.

"After all," he thought, "my only object in killing them was to prevent their carrying news of my monstrous appearance to the outside world; so if I can but manage to keep them forever in my kingdom it will answer my purpose equally well."

As the result of this thought he presently raised his head and spoke to Prince Marvel in a quiet and even cheerful voice.

"Enough of these rude and boisterous games," said he, with a smile that showed his white teeth in a repulsive manner. "They may have seemed to my people an ill welcome to my good friend, Prince Marvel; yet they were only designed to show the powers of the mighty magician who has become my guest. Nay, do not deny it, Prince; from the first I guessed your secret, and to prove myself right I called my servants to oppose you, being sure they could not do you an injury. But no more of such fooling, and pray forgive my merry game at your expense. Henceforth we shall be friends, and you are heartily welcome to the best my kingdom affords."

With this speech Terribus stepped down from his throne and approached Prince Marvel with outstretched hand. The prince was not at all deceived, but he was pleased to see how cunningly the king excused his attempts to kill him. So he laughed and touched the hand Terribus extended, for this fairy prince seemed to have no anger against any mortal who ventured to oppose him.

The strangers were now conducted, with every mark of respect, to a beautiful suite of apartments in the castle, wherein were soft beds with velvet spreads, marble baths with perfumed waters, and a variety of silken and brocaded costumes from which they might select a change of raiment.

No sooner had they bathed and adorned themselves fittingly than they were summoned to the king's banquet hall, being escorted thither by twelve young maidens bearing torches with lavender-colored flames.

The night had fallen upon the mountains outside, but the great banquet hall was brilliant with the glow of a thousand candles, and seated at the head of the long table was King Terribus.

Yet here, as in the throne-room, the ruler of Spor was dressed in simplest garments, and his seat was a rough block of stone. All about him were lords and ladies in gorgeous array; the walls were hung with rare embroideries; the table was weighted with gold platters and richly carved goblets filled with sweet nectars. But the king himself, with his horrid, ugly head, was like a great blot on a fair parchment, and even Prince Marvel could not repress a shudder as he gazed upon him.

Terribus placed his guest upon his right hand and loaded him with honors. Nerle stood behind the prince's chair and served him faithfully, as an esquire should. But the other servants treated Nerle with much deference, noting in him an air of breeding that marked him the unusual servant of an unusual master.

Indeed, most curious were the looks cast on these marvelous men who had calmly walked into the castle of mighty Terribus and successfully defied his anger; for in spite of his youthful appearance and smiling face every attendant at the banquet feared Prince Marvel even more than they feared their own fierce king.

Chapter 11 - The Cunning of King Terribus

The days that followed were pleasant ones for Prince Marvel and Nerle, who were treated as honored guests by both the king and his courtiers. But the prince seemed to be the favorite, for at all games of skill and trials at arms he was invariably the victor, while in the evenings, when the grand ball-room was lighted up and the musicians played sweet music, none was so graceful in the dance as the fairy prince.

Nerle soon tired of the games and dancing, for he had been accustomed to them at his father's castle; and moreover he was shy in the society of ladies; so before many weeks had passed he began to mope and show a discontented face.

One day the prince noticed his esquire's dismal expression of countenance, and asked the cause of it.

"Why," said Nerle, "here I have left my home to seek worries and troubles, and have found but the same humdrum life that existed at my father's castle. Here our days are made smooth and pleasant, and there is no excitement or grief, whatever. You have become a carpet-knight, Prince Marvel, and think more of bright eyes than of daring deeds. So, if you will release me from your service I will seek further adventures."

"Nay," returned the prince, "we will go together; for I, too, am tired of this life of pleasure."

So next morning Marvel sought the presence of King Terribus and said:

"I have come to bid your Majesty adieu, for my esquire and I are about to leave your dominions."

At first the king laughed, and his long nose began to sway from side to side. Then, seeing the prince was in earnest, his Majesty frowned and grew disturbed. Finally he said:

"I must implore you to remain my guests a short time longer. No one has ever before visited me in my mountain home, and I do not wish to lose the pleasure of your society so soon."

"Nevertheless, we must go," answered the prince, briefly.

"Are you not contented?" asked Terribus. "Ask whatever you may desire, and it shall be granted you."

"We desire adventures amid new scenes," said Marvel, "and these you can not give us except by permission to depart."

Seeing his guest was obstinate the king ceased further argument and said:

"Very well; go if you wish. But I shall hope to see you return to us this evening."

The prince paid no heed to this peculiar speech, but left the hall and hurried to the courtyard of the castle, where Nerle was holding the horses in readiness for their journey.

Standing around were many rows and files of the Gray Men, and when they reached the marble roadway they found it lined with motionless forms of the huge giants. But no one interfered with them in any way, although both Prince Marvel and Nerle knew that every eye followed them as they rode forward.

Curiously enough, they had both forgotten from what direction they had approached the castle; for, whereas they had at that time noticed but one marble roadway leading to the entrance, they now saw that there were several of these, each one connecting with a path through the mountains.

"It really doesn't matter which way we go, so long as we get away from the Kingdom of Spor," said Prince Marvel; so he selected a path by chance, and soon they were riding through a mountain pass.

The pleased, expectant look on Nerle's face had gradually turned to one of gloom.

"I hoped we should have a fight to get away," he said, sadly; "and in that case I might have suffered considerable injury and pain. But no one has injured us in any way, and perhaps King Terribus is really glad to be rid of us."

"With good reason, too, if such is the case," laughed Marvel; "for, mark you, Nerle, the king has discovered we are more powerful than he is, and had he continued to oppose us, we might have destroyed his entire army."

On they rode through the rough hill paths, winding this way and that, until they lost all sense of the direction in which they were going.

"Never mind," said the prince; "so long as we get farther and farther away from the ugly Terribus I shall be satisfied."

"Perhaps we are getting into more serious danger than ever," answered Nerle, brightening; "one of the giants told me the other day that near the foot of these mountains is the Kingdom of the High Ki of Twi."

"Who is the High Ki of Twi?" asked Prince Marvel.

"No one knows," answered Nerle.

"And what is the Kingdom of Twi like?"

"No one knows that," answered Nerle.

"Then," returned the prince, with a smile, "if by chance we visit the place we shall know more than any one else."

At noon they ate luncheon by the wayside, Nerle having filled his pouch by stealth at the breakfast table. There were great fragments of rock lying all about them, and the sun beat down so fiercely that the heat reflected from the rocks was hard to bear. So the travelers did not linger over their meal, but remounted and rode away as soon as possible. When the sun began to get lower in the sky the rocks beside the path threw the riders into shadow, so that their journey became more pleasant. They rode along, paying little attention to the way, but talking and laughing merrily together, until it began to grow dark.

"Does this path never end?" asked Prince Marvel, suddenly. "We ought to reach some place where men dwell before long, else we shall be obliged to spend the night among these rocks."

"And then perhaps the wolves will attack us," said Nerle, cheerfully, "and tear us into pieces with their sharp teeth and claws."

But even as he spoke they rode around a turn in the path and saw a sight that made them pause in astonishment. For just before them rose the castle of King Terribus, and along both sides of the marble walk leading up to it were ranged the lines of giants, exactly as they had stood in the morning.

Nerle turned around in his saddle. Sure enough, there were the Gray Men in the rear, stepping from behind every boulder and completely filling the rocky pathway.

"Well, what shall we do?" asked the esquire; "fight?"

"No, indeed!" returned Prince Marvel, laughing at his friend's eager face. "It appears the path we chose winds around in a circle, and so has brought us back to our starting-point. So we must make the best of a bad blunder and spend another night with our ugly friend King Terribus."

They rode forward through the rows of giants to the castle, where the ever-courteous servants took their horses and escorted them to their former handsome apartments with every mark of respect.

No one seemed in the least surprised at their speedy return, and this fact at first puzzled Nerle, and then made him suspicious.

After bathing and dusting their clothing they descended to the banquet hall, where King Terribus sat upon his gray stone throne and welcomed them with quiet courtesy.

The sight of the king's crimson skin and deformed face sent a thrill of repugnance through Prince Marvel, and under the impulse of a sudden thought he extended his hand toward Terribus and whispered a magic word which was unheard by any around him.

Nerle did not notice the prince's swift gesture nor the whispered word; but he was staring straight at Terribus at the time, and he saw with surprise the eye on the top of the king's head move down toward his forehead, and the eye in the center of his forehead slide slightly toward the left, and the elephant-like nose shrink and shorten at the same time. Also it seemed to him that the king's skin was not so crimson in color as before, and that a thin growth of hair had covered his head.

However, no one else appeared to notice any change, least of all Terribus, so Nerle seated himself at the table and began to eat.

"It was very kind of you to return so soon to my poor castle," said the king to Prince Marvel, in his sweet voice.

"We could not help it," laughed the prince, in reply; "for the road wound right and left until we knew not which way we traveled; and then it finally circled around again to your castle. But to-morrow we shall seek a new path and bid you farewell forever."

"Still," remarked the king, gravely, "should you again miss your way, I shall be glad to welcome your return."

The prince bowed politely by way of reply, and turned to address the little maiden he had once saved from death by poison. And so in feasting, dancing and laughter the evening passed pleasantly enough to the prince, and it was late when he called Nerle to attend him to their apartment.

Chapter 12 - The Gift of Beauty

The following morning Marvel and Nerle once more set out to leave the Kingdom of Spor and its ugly king. They selected another pathway leading from the castle and traveled all day, coming at nightfall into view of the place whence they had started, with its solemn rows of giants and Gray Men standing ready to receive them.

This repetition of their former experience somewhat annoyed the prince, while Nerle's usually despondent face wore a smile.

"I see trouble ahead," murmured the esquire, almost cheerfully. "Since the king can not conquer us by force he intends to do it by sorcery."

Marvel did not reply, but greeted the king quietly, while Terribus welcomed their return as calmly as if he well knew they could not escape him.

That evening the prince made another pass toward the king with his hand and muttered again the magic word. Nerle was watching, and saw the upper eye of Terribus glide still farther down his forehead and the other eye move again toward the left. The swaying nose shrank to a few inches in length, and the skin that had once been so brilliantly crimson turned to a dull red color. This time the courtiers and ladies in waiting also noticed the change in the king's features, but were afraid to speak of it, as any reference to their monarch's personal appearance was by law punishable by death. Terribus saw the startled looks directed upon him, and raised his hand to feel of his nose and eyes; but thinking that if any change in his appearance had taken place, he must be uglier than before, he only frowned and turned away his head.

The next day the king's guests made a third attempt to leave his dominions, but met with no better success than before, for a long and tedious ride only brought them back to their starting-place in the evening.

This time Prince Marvel was really angry, and striding into the king's presence he reproached him bitterly, saying:

"Why do you prevent us from leaving your kingdom? We have not injured you in any way."

"You have seen ME, returned Terribus, calmly, "and I do not intend you shall go back to the world and tell people how ugly I am."

The prince looked at him, and could not repress a smile. The two eyes of the king, having been twice removed from their first position, were now both in his forehead, instead of below it, and one was much higher than the other. And the nose, although small when compared to what it had been, still resembled an elephant's trunk. Other changes had been made for the better, but Terribus was still exceedingly repulsive to look upon.

Seeing the prince look at him and smile, the king flew into a fury of anger and declared that the strangers should never, while they lived, be permitted to leave his castle again. Prince Marvel became thoughtful at this, reflecting that the king's enmity all arose from his sensitiveness about his ugly appearance, and this filled the youthful knight with pity rather than resentment.

When they had all assembled at the evening banquet the prince, for a third time, made a mystic pass at the king and whispered a magic word. And behold! this time the charm was complete. For the two front eyes of Terribus fell into their proper places, his nose became straight and well formed, and his skin took on a natural, healthy color. Moreover, he now had a fine head of soft brown hair, with eyebrows and eyelashes to match, and his head was shapely and in proportion to his body. As for the eye that had formerly been in the back of his head, it had disappeared completely.

So amazed were the subjects of the transformed king, who was now quite handsome to look upon, that they began to murmur together excitedly, and something in the new sensations he experienced gave to the king's face likewise an expression of surprise. Knowing from their pleased looks that he must have improved in appearance, he found courage to raise his hand to his nose, and found it well formed. Then he touched his eyes, and realized they were looking straight out from his face, like those of other people.

For some moments after making these discoveries the king remained motionless, a smile of joy gradually spreading over his features. Then he said, aloud:

"What has happened? Why do you all look so startled?"

"Your Majesty is no longer ugly," replied Marvel, laughingly; "so that when Nerle and I leave your kingdom we can proclaim nothing less than praise of your dignified and handsome appearance."

"Is my face indeed pleasing?" demanded the king, eagerly.

"It is!" cried the assembled courtiers and ladies, as with one voice.

"Bring me a mirror!" said the king. "I shall look at my reflection for the first time in many years."

The mirror being brought King Terribus regarded himself for a long time with pleased astonishment; and then, his sensitive nature being overcome by the shock of his good fortune, he burst into a flood of tears and rushed from the room.

The courtiers and ladies now bestowed many grateful thanks upon Prince Marvel for his kind deed; for they realized that thereafter their lives would be safer from the king's anger and much pleasanter in every way.

"Terribus is not bad by nature," said one; "but he brooded upon his ugliness so much that the least thing served to throw him into a violent passion, and our lives were never safe from one day to another."

By and by two giants entered the hall and carried away the throne of gray stone where Terribus had been accustomed to sit; and other slaves brought a gorgeous throne of gold, studded with precious jewels, which they put in its place. And after a time the king himself returned to the room, his simple gray gown replaced by flowing robes of purple, with rich embroideries, such as he had not worn for many years.

"My people," said he, addressing those present with kindness and dignity, "it seems to me fitting that a handsome king should be handsomely attired, and an ugly one clothed simply. For years I have been so terrible in feature that I dared not even look at my own image in a mirror. But now, thanks to the gracious magic of my guest, I have become like other men, and hereafter you will find my rule as kind as it was formerly cruel. To-night, in honor of this joyous occasion, we shall feast and make merry, and it is my royal command that you all do honor and reverence to the illustrious Prince Marvel!"

A loud shout of approval greeted this speech, and the evening was merry indeed. Terribus joined freely in the revelry, laughing as gaily as the lightest-hearted damsel present.

It was nearly morning before they all retired, and as they sought their beds Nerle asked the prince in a voice that sounded like an ill-natured growl:

"Why did you give the king beauty, after his treatment of us?"

Marvel looked at the reproachful face of his esquire and smiled. "When you are older," said he, "you will find that often there are many ways to accomplish a single purpose. The king's ugliness was the bar to our leaving his country, for he feared our gossip. So the easiest way for us to compass our escape was to take away his reason for detaining us. Thus I conquered the king in my own way, and at the same time gained his gratitude and friendship."

"Will he allow us to depart in the morning?" inquired Nerle.

"I think so," said Marvel.

It was late when they rose from their slumbers; but, having breakfasted, the prince's first act was to seek the king.

"We wish to leave your kingdom," said he. "Will you let us go?"

Terribus grasped the hand of his guest and pressed it with fervor, while tears of gratitude stood in his eyes.

"I should prefer that you remain with me always, and be my friend," he answered. "But if you choose to leave me I shall not interfere in any way with your wishes."

Prince Marvel looked at him thoughtfully, and then said: "My time on this island is short. In a few months Prince Marvel will have passed out of the knowledge of men, and his name will be forgotten. Before then I hope to visit the Kingdoms of Dawna and Auriel and Plenta; so I must not delay, but beg you will permit me to depart at once."

"Very well," answered Terribus. "Come with me, and I shall show you the way."

He led the prince and Nerle to a high wall of rock, and placing his hand upon its rough surface, touched a hidden spring. Instantly an immense block of stone began to swing backward, disclosing a passage large enough for a man on horseback to ride through.

"This is the one road that leads out of my kingdom," said Terribus. "The others all begin and end at the castle. So that unless you know the secret of this passage you could never escape from Spor."

"But where does this road lead?" asked Marvel.

"To the Kingdom of Auriel, which you desire to visit. It is not a straight road, for it winds around the Land of Twi, so it will carry you a little out of your way."

"What is the Land of Twi?" inquired the prince.

"A small country hidden from the view of all travelers," said Terribus. "No one has ever yet found a way to enter the land of Twi; yet there is a rumor that it is ruled by a mighty personage called the High Ki."

"And does the rumor state what the High Ki of Twi is like?"

"No, indeed," returned the king, smiling, "so it will do you no good to be curious. And now farewell, and may good luck attend you. Yet bear in mind the fact that King Terribus of Spor owes you a mighty debt of gratitude; and if you ever need my services, you have but to call on me, and I shall gladly come to your assistance."

"I thank you," said Marvel, "but there is small chance of my needing help. Farewell, and may your future life be pleasant and happy!"

With this he sprang to the saddle of his prancing charger and, followed by Nerle, rode slowly through the stone arch. The courtiers and ladies had flocked from the palace to witness their departure, and the giants and dwarfs and Gray Men were drawn up in long lines to speed the king's guests. So it was a brilliant sight that Marvel and Nerle looked back on; but once they were clear of the arch, the great stone rolled back into its place, shutting them out completely from the Kingdom of Spor, with its turreted castle and transformed king.

Chapter 13 - The Hidden Kingdom of Twi

Knowing that at last they were free to roam according to their desire, the travelers rode gaily along the paths, taking but scant heed of their way.

"Our faces are set toward new adventures," remarked the prince. "Let us hope they will prove more pleasant than the last."

"To be sure!" responded Nerle. "Let us hope, at any rate, that we shall suffer more privations and encounter more trouble than we did in that mountainous Kingdom of Spor." Then he added: "For one reason, I regret you are my master."

"What is that reason?" asked the prince, turning to smile upon his esquire.

"You have a way of overcoming all difficulties without any trouble whatsoever, and that deprives me of any chance of coming to harm while in your company."

"Cheer up, my boy!" cried Marvel. "Did I not say there are new adventures before us? We may not come through them so easily as we came through the others."

"That is true," replied Nerle; "it is always best to hope." And then he inquired: "Why do you stop here, in the middle of the path?"

"Because the path has ended rather suddenly," answered Marvel. "Here is a thick hedge of prickly briers barring our way."

Nerle looked over his master's shoulder and saw that a great hedge, high and exceedingly thick, cut off all prospect of their advancing.

"This is pleasant," said he; "but I might try to force our way through the hedge. The briers would probably prick me severely, and that would be delightful."

"Try it!" the prince returned, with twinkling eyes.

Nerle sprang from his horse to obey, but at the first contact with the briers he uttered a howl of pain and held up his hands, which were bleeding in a dozen places from the wounds of the thorns.

"Ah, that will content you for a time, I trust," said Marvel. "Now follow me, and we will ride along beside the hedge until we find an opening. For either it will come to an end or there will prove to be a way through it to the other side."

So they rode alongside the hedge for hour after hour; yet it did not end, nor could they espy any way to get through the thickly matted briers. By and by night fell, and they tethered their horses to some shrubs, where there were a few scanty blades of grass for them to crop, and then laid themselves down upon the ground, with bare rocks for pillows, where they managed to sleep soundly until morning.

They had brought a supply of food in their pouches, and on this they breakfasted, afterward continuing their journey beside the hedge.

At noon Prince Marvel uttered an exclamation of surprise and stopped his horse.

"What is it?" asked Nerle.

"I have found the handkerchief with which you wiped the blood from your hands yesterday morning, and then carelessly dropped," replied the prince. "This proves that we have made a complete circle around this hedge without finding a way to pass through it."

"In that case," said Nerle, "we had better leave the hedge and go in another direction."

"Not so," declared Marvel. "The hedge incloses some unknown country, and I am curious to find out what it is."

"But there is no opening," remonstrated Nerle.

"Then we must make one. Wouldn't you like to enjoy a little more pain?"

"Thank you," answered Nerle, "my hands are still smarting very comfortably from the pricks of yesterday."

"Therefore I must make the attempt myself," said the prince, and drawing his sword he whispered a queer word to it, and straightway began slashing at the hedge.

The brambles fell fast before his blade, and when he had cut a big heap of branches from the hedge Nerle dragged them to one side, and the prince began again.

It was marvelous how thick the hedge proved. Only a magic sword could have done this work and remained sharp, and only a fairy arm could have proved strong enough to hew through the tough wood. But the magic sword and fairy arm were at work, and naught could resist them.

After a time the last branches were severed and dragged from the path, and then the travelers rode their horses through the gap into the unknown country beyond.

They saw at first glance that it was a land of great beauty; but after that one look both Prince Marvel and Nerle paused and rubbed their eyes, to assure themselves that their vision was not blurred.

Before them were two trees, exactly alike. And underneath the trees two cows were grazing, each a perfect likeness of the other. At their left were two cottages, with every door and window and chimney the exact counterpart of another. Before these houses two little boys were playing, evidently twins, for they not only looked alike and dressed alike, but every motion one made was also made by the other at the same time and in precisely the same way. When one laughed the other laughed, and when one stubbed his toe and fell down, the other did likewise, and then they both sat up and cried lustily at the same time.

At this two women, it was impossible to tell one from the other, rushed out of the two houses, caught up the two boys, shook and dusted them in precisely the same way, and led them by their ears back into the houses.

Again the astonished travelers rubbed their eyes, and then Prince Marvel looked at Nerle and said:

"I thought at first that I saw everything double, but there seems to be only one of YOU."

"And of you," answered the boy. "But see! there are two hills ahead of us, and two paths lead from the houses over the hills! How strange it all is!"

Just then two birds flew by, close together and perfect mates; and the cows raised their heads and "mooed" at the same time; and two men, also twins, came over the two hills along the two paths with two dinner-pails in their hands and entered the two houses. They were met at the doors by the two women, who kissed them exactly at the same time and helped them off with their coats with the same motions, and closed the two doors with two slams at the same instant.

Nerle laughed. "What sort of country have we got into?" he asked.

"Let us find out," replied the prince, and riding up to one of the houses he knocked on the door with the hilt of his sword.

Instantly the doors of both houses flew open, and both men appeared in the doorways. Both started back in amazement at sight of the strangers, and both women shrieked and both little boys began to cry. Both mothers boxed the children's ears, and both men gasped out:

"Who, who are you?"

Their voices were exactly alike, and their words were spoken in unison. Prince Marvel replied, courteously:

"We are two strangers who have strayed into your country. But I do not understand why our appearance should so terrify you."

"Why, you are singular! There is only half of each of you!" exclaimed the two men, together.

"Not so," said the prince, trying hard not to laugh in their faces. "We may be single, while you appear to be double; but each of us is perfect, nevertheless."

"Perfect! And only half of you!" cried the men. And again the two women, who were looking over their husbands' shoulders, screamed at sight of the strangers; and again the two boys, who were clinging to their mothers' dresses in the same positions, began to cry.

"We did not know such strange people existed!" said the two men, both staring at the strangers and then wiping the beads of perspiration from their two brows with two faded yellow handkerchiefs.

"Nor did we!" retorted the prince. "I assure you we are as much surprised as you are."

Nerle laughed again at this, and to hear only one of the strangers speak and the other only laugh seemed to terrify the double people anew. So Prince Marvel quickly asked:

"Please tell us what country this is?"

"The Land of Twi," answered both men, together.

"Oh! the Land of Twi. And why is the light here so dim?" continued the prince.

"Dim?" repeated the men, as if surprised; "why, this is twilight, of course."

"Of course," said Nerle. "I hadn't thought of that. We are in the long hidden Land of Twi, which all men have heard of, but no man has found before."

"And who may you be?" questioned the prince, looking from one man to the other, curiously.

"We are Twis," they answered.

"Twice?"

"Twis - inhabitants of Twi."

"It's the same thing," laughed Nerle. "You see everything twice in this land."

"Are none of your people single?" asked Prince Marvel.

"Single," returned the men, as if perplexed. "We don't understand."

"Are you all double? or are some of you just one?" said the prince, who found it difficult to put his question plainly.

"What does 'one' mean?" asked the men. "There is no such word as 'one' in our language."

"They have no need of such a word," declared Nerle.

"We are only poor laborers," explained the men. "But over the hills lie the cities of Twi, where the Ki and the Ki-Ki dwell, and also the High Ki."

"Ah!" said Marvel, "I've heard of your High Ki. Who is he?"

The men shook their heads, together and with the same motion.

"We have never seen the glorious High Ki," they answered. "The sight of their faces is forbidden. None but the Ki and the Ki-Ki has seen the Supreme Rulers and High Ki."

"I'm getting mixed," said Nerle. "All this about the Ki and the Ki-Ki and the High Ki makes me dizzy. Let's go on to the city and explore it."

"That is a good suggestion," replied the prince. "Good by, my friends," he added, addressing the men.

They both bowed, and although they still seemed somewhat frightened they answered him civilly and in the same words, and closed their doors at the same time.

So Prince Marvel and Nerle rode up the double path to the hills, and the two cows became frightened and ran away with the same swinging step, keeping an exact space apart. And when they were a safe distance they both stopped, looked over their right shoulders, and "mooed" at the same instant.

Chapter 14 - The Ki and the Ki-Ki

From the tops of the hills the travelers caught their first glimpse of the wonderful cities of Twi. Two walls surrounded the cities, and in the walls were two gates just alike. Within the inclosures stood many houses, but all were built in pairs, from the poorest huts to the most splendid palaces. Every street was double, the pavements running side by side. There were two lamp-posts on every corner, and in the dim twilight that existed these lamp-posts were quite necessary. If there were trees or bushes anywhere, they invariably grew in pairs, and if a branch was broken on one it was sure to be broken on the other, and dead leaves fell from both trees at identically the same moment.

Much of this Marvel and Nerle learned after they had entered the cities, but the view from the hills showed plainly enough that the "double" plan existed everywhere and in every way in this strange land.

They followed the paths down to the gates of the walls, where two pairs of soldiers rushed out and seized their horses by the bridles. These soldiers all seemed to be twins, or at least mates, and each one of each pair was as like the other as are two peas growing in the same pod. If one had a red nose the other's was red in the same degree, and the soldiers that held the bridles of Nerle's horse both had their left eyes bruised and blackened, as from a blow of the same force.

These soldiers, as they looked upon Nerle and the prince, seemed fully as much astonished and certainly more frightened than their prisoners. They were dressed in bright yellow uniforms with green buttons, and the soldiers who had arrested the prince had both torn their left coat-sleeves and had patches of the same shape upon the seats of their trousers.

"How dare you stop us, fellows?" asked the prince, sternly.

The soldiers holding his horse both turned and looked inquiringly at the soldiers holding Nerle's horse; and these turned to look at a double captain who came out of two doors in the wall and walked up to them.

"Such things were never before heard of!" said the two captains, their startled eyes fixed upon the prisoners. "We must take them to the Ki and the Ki-Ki."

"Why so?" asked Prince Marvel.

"Because," replied the officers, "they are our rulers, under grace of the High Ki, and all unusual happenings must be brought to their notice. It is our law, you know, the law of the Kingdom of Twi."

"Very well," said Marvel, quietly; "take us where you will; but if any harm is intended us you will be made to regret it."

"The Ki and the Ki-Ki will decide," returned the captains gravely, their words sounding at the same instant.

And then the two pairs of soldiers led the horses through the double streets, the captains marching ahead with drawn swords, and crowds of twin men and twin women coming from the double doors of the double houses to gaze upon the strange sight of men and horses who were not double.

Presently they came upon a twin palace with twin turrets rising high into the air; and before the twin doors the prisoners dismounted. Marvel was escorted through one door and Nerle through another, and then they saw each other going down a double hallway to a room with a double entrance.

Passing through this they found themselves in a large hall with two domes set side by side in the roof. The domes were formed of stained glass, and the walls of the hall were ornamented by pictures in pairs, each pair showing identically the same scenes. This, was, of course, reasonable enough in such a land, where two people would always look at two pictures at the same time and admire them in the same way with the same thoughts.

Beneath one of the domes stood a double throne, on which sat the Ki of Twi, a pair of gray-bearded and bald-headed men who were lean and lank and stoop-shouldered. They had small eyes, black and flashing, long hooked noses, great pointed ears, and they were smoking two pipes from which the smoke curled in exactly the same circles and clouds.

Beneath the other dome sat the Ki-Ki of Twi, also on double thrones, similar to those of the Ki. The Ki-Ki were two young men, and had golden hair combed over their brows and "banged" straight across; and their eyes were blue and mild in expression, and their cheeks pink and soft. The Ki-Ki were playing softly upon a pair of musical instruments that resembled mandolins, and they were evidently trying to learn a new piece of music, for when one Ki-Ki struck a false note the other Ki-Ki struck the same false note at the same time, and the same expression of annoyance came over the two faces at the same moment.

When the prisoners entered, the pairs of captains and soldiers bowed low to the two pairs of rulers, and the Ki exclaimed, both in the same voice of surprise:

"Great Kika-koo! what have we here?"

"Most wonderful prisoners, your Highnesses," answered the captains. "We found them at your cities' gates and brought them to you at once. They are, as your Highnesses will see, each singular, and but half of what he should be."

"'Tis so!" cried the double Ki, in loud voices, and slapping their right thighs with their right palms at the same time. "Most remarkable! Most remarkable!"

"I don't see anything remarkable about it," returned Prince Marvel, calmly. "It is you, who are not singular, but double, that seem strange and outlandish."

"Perhaps, perhaps!" said the two old men, thoughtfully. "It is what we are not accustomed to that seems to us remarkable. Eh, Ki-Ki?" they added, turning to the other rulers.

The Ki-Ki, who had not spoken a word but continued to play softly, simply nodded their blond heads carelessly; so the Ki looked again at the prisoners and asked:

"How did you get here?"

"We cut a hole through the prickly hedge," replied Prince Marvel.

"A hole through the hedge! Great Kika-koo!" cried the gray-bearded Ki; "is there, then, anything or any place on the other side of the hedge?"

"Why, of course! The world is there," returned the prince, laughing.

The old men looked puzzled, and glanced sharply from their little black eyes at their prisoners.

"We thought nothing existed outside the hedge of Twi," they answered, simply. "But your presence here proves we were wrong. Eh! Ki-Ki?"

This last was again directed toward the pair of musicians, who continued to play and only nodded quietly, as before.

"Now that you are here," said the twin Ki, stroking their two gray beards with their two left hands in a nervous way, "it must be evident to you that you do not belong here. Therefore you must go back through the hedge again and stay on the other side. Eh, Ki-Ki?"

The Ki-Ki still continued playing, but now spoke the first words the prisoners had heard from them.

"They must die," said the Ki-Ki, in soft and agreeable voices.

"Die!" echoed the twin Ki, "die? Great Kika-koo! And why so?"

"Because, if there is a world on the other side of the hedge, they would tell on their return all about the Land of Twi, and others of their kind would come through the hedge from curiosity and annoy us. We can not be annoyed. We are busy."

Having delivered this speech both the Ki-Ki went on playing the new tune, as if the matter was settled.

"Nonsense!" retorted the old Ki, angrily. "You are getting more and more bloodthirsty every day, our sweet and gentle Ki-Ki! But we are the Ki, and we say the prisoners shall not die!"

"We say they shall!" answered the youthful Ki-Ki, nodding their two heads at the same time, with a positive motion. "You may be the Ki, but we are the Ki-Ki, and your superior."

"Not in this case," declared the old men. "Where life and death are concerned we have equal powers with you."

"And if we disagree?" asked the players, gently.

"Great Kika-koo! If we disagree the High Ki must judge between us!" roared the twin Ki, excitedly.

"Quite so," answered the Ki-Ki. "The strangers shall die."

"They shall not die!" stormed the old men, with fierce gestures toward the others, while both pairs of black eyes flashed angrily.

"Then we disagree, and they must be taken to the High Ki," returned the blond musicians, beginning to play another tune.

The two Ki rose from their thrones, paced two steps to the right and three steps to the left, and then sat down again.

"Very well!" they said to the captains, who had listened unmoved to the quarrel of the rulers; "keep these half-men safe prisoners until to-morrow morning, and then the Ki-Ki and we ourselves will conduct them to the mighty High Ki."

At this command the twin captains bowed again to both pairs of rulers and led Prince Marvel and Nerle from the room. Then they were escorted along the streets to the twin houses of the captains, and here the officers paused and scratched their left ears with uncertain gestures.

"There being only half of each of you," they said, "we do not know how to lock each of you in double rooms."

"Oh, let us both occupy the same room," said Prince Marvel. "We prefer it."

"Very well," answered the captains; "we must transgress our usual customs in any event, so you may as well be lodged as you wish."

So Nerle and the prince were thrust into a large and pleasant room of one of the twin houses, the double doors were locked upon them by twin soldiers, and they were left to their own thoughts.

Chapter 15 - The High Ki of Twi

"Tell me, Prince, are we awake or asleep?" asked Nerle, as soon as they were alone.

"There is no question of our being awake," replied the prince, with a laugh. "But what a curious country it is and what a funny people!"

"We can't call them odd or singular," said the esquire, "for everything is even in numbers and double in appearance. It makes me giddy to look at them, and I keep feeling of myself to make sure there is still only one of me."

"You are but half a boy!" laughed the prince "at least so long as you remain in the Land of Twi."

"I'd like to get out of it in double-quick time," answered Nerle; "and we should even now be on the other side of the hedge were it not for that wicked pair of Ki-Ki, who are determined to kill us."

"It is strange," said the prince, thoughtfully, "that the fierce-looking old Ki should be our friends and the gentle Ki-Ki our enemies. How little one can tell from appearances what sort of heart beats in a person's body!"

Before Nerle could answer the two doors opened and two pairs of soldiers entered. They drew two small tables before the prince and two before Nerle, and then other pairs of twin soldiers came and spread cloths on the tables and set twin platters of meat and bread and fruit on each of the tables. When the meal had been arranged the prisoners saw that there was enough for four people instead of two; and the soldiers realized this also, for they turned puzzled looks first on the tables and then on the prisoners. Then they shook all their twin heads gravely and went away, locking the twin doors behind them.

"We have one advantage in being singular," said Nerle, cheerfully; "and that is we are not likely to starve to death. For we can eat the portions of our missing twins as well as our own."

"I should think you would enjoy starving," remarked the prince.

"No; I believe I have more exquisite suffering in store for me, since I have met that gentle pair of Ki-Ki," said Nerle.

While they were eating the two captains came in and sat down in two chairs. These captains seemed friendly fellows, and after watching the strangers for a while they remarked:

"We are glad to see you able to eat so heartily; for to-morrow you will probably die."

"That is by no means certain," replied Marvel, cutting a piece from one of the twin birds on a platter before him, to the extreme surprise of the captains, who had always before seen both birds carved alike at the same time. "Your gray-bearded old Ki say we shall not die."

"True," answered the captains. "But the Ki-Ki have declared you shall."

"Their powers seem to be equal," said Nerle, "and we are to be taken before the High Ki for judgment."

"Therein lies your danger," returned the captains, speaking in the same tones and with the same accents on their words. "For it is well known the Ki-Ki has more influence with the High Ki than the Ki has."

"Hold on!" cried Nerle; "you are making me dizzy again. I can't keep track of all these Kis."

"What is the High Ki like?" asked Prince Marvel, who was much interested in the conversation of the captains. But this question the officers seemed unable to answer. They shook their heads slowly and said:

"The High Ki are not visible to the people of Twi. Only in cases of the greatest importance are the High Ki ever bothered or even approached by the Ki and the Ki-Ki, who are supposed to rule the land according to their own judgment. But if they chance to disagree, then the matter is carried before the High Ki, who live in a palace surrounded by high walls, in which there are no gates. Only these rulers have ever seen the other side of the walls, or know what the High Ki are like."

"That is strange," said the prince. "But we, ourselves, it seems, are to see the High Ki tomorrow, and whoever they may chance to be, we hope to remain alive after the interview."

"That is a vain hope," answered the captains, "for it is well known that the High Ki usually decide in favor of the Ki-Ki, and against the wishes of the old Ki."

"That is certainly encouraging," said Nerle.

When the captains had gone and left them to themselves, the esquire confided to his master his expectations in the following speech:

"This High Ki sounds something terrible and fierce in my ears, and as they are doubtless a pair, they will be twice terrible and fierce. Perhaps his royal doublets will torture me most exquisitely before putting me to death, and then I shall feel that I have not lived in vain."

They slept in comfortable beds that night, although an empty twin bed stood beside each one they occupied. And in the morning they were served another excellent meal, after which the captains escorted them again to the twin palaces of the Ki and the Ki-Ki.

There the two pairs of rulers met them and headed the long procession of soldiers toward the palace of the High Ki. First came a band of music, in which many queer sorts of instruments were played in pairs by twin musicians; and it was amusing to Nerle to see the twin drummers roll their twin drums exactly at the same time and the twin trumpets peal out twin notes. After the band marched the double Ki-Ki and the double Ki, their four bodies side by side in a straight line. The Ki-Ki had left their musical instruments in the palace, and now wore yellow gloves with green stitching down the backs and swung gold-headed canes jauntily as they walked. The Ki stooped their aged shoulders and shuffled along with their hands in their pockets, and only once did they speak, and that was to roar "Great Kika-koo!" when the Ki-Ki jabbed their canes down on the Ki's toes.

Following the Ki-Ki and the Ki came the prince and Nerle, escorted by the twin captains, and then there were files of twin soldiers bringing up the rear.

Crowds of twin people, with many twin children amongst them, turned out to watch the unusual display, and many pairs of twin dogs barked together in unison and snapped at the heels of the marching twin soldiers.

By and by they reached the great wall surrounding the High Ki's palace, and, sure enough, there was never a gate in the wall by which any might enter. But when the Ki and the Ki-Ki had blown a shrill signal upon two pairs of whistles, they all beheld two flights of silver steps begin to descend from the top of the wall, and these came nearer and nearer the ground until at last they rested at the feet of the Ki. Then the old men began ascending the steps carefully and slowly, and the captains motioned to the prisoners to follow. So Prince Marvel followed one of the Ki up the steps and Nerle the other Ki, while the two Ki-Ki came behind them so they could not escape.

So to the top of the wall they climbed, where a pair of twin servants in yellow and green, which seemed to be the royal colors, welcomed them and drew up the pair of silver steps, afterward letting them down on the other side of the wall, side by side.

They descended in the same order as they had mounted to the top of the wall, and now Prince Marvel and Nerle found themselves in a most beautiful garden, filled with twin beds of twin flowers, with many pairs of rare shrubs. Also, there were several double statuettes on pedestals, and double fountains sending exactly the same sprays of water the same distance into the air.

Double walks ran in every direction through the garden, and in the center of the inclosure stood a magnificent twin palace, built of blocks of white marble exquisitely carved.

The Ki and the Ki-Ki at once led their prisoners toward the palace and entered at its large arched double doors, where several pairs of servants met them. These servants, they found, were all dumb, so that should they escape from the palace walls they could tell no tales of the High Ki.

The prisoners now proceeded through several pairs of halls, winding this way and that, and at last came to a pair of golden double doors leading into the throne-room of the mighty High Ki. Here they all paused, and the Ki-Ki both turned to the prince and Nerle and said:

"You are the only persons, excepting ourselves and the palace servants, who have ever been permitted to see the High Ki of Twi. As you are about to die, that does not matter; but should you by any chance be permitted to live, you must never breathe a word of what you are about to see, under penalty of a sure and horrible death."

The prisoners made no reply to this speech, and, after the two Ki-Ki had given them another mild look from their gentle blue eyes, these officials clapped their twin hands together and the doors of gold flew open.

A perfect silence greeted them, during which the double Ki and the double Ki-Ki bent their four bodies low and advanced into the throne-room, followed by Prince Marvel and Nerle.

In the center of the room stood two thrones of dainty filigree work in solid gold, and over them were canopies of yellow velvet, the folds of which were caught up and draped with bands of green ribbon. And on the thrones were seated two of the sweetest and fairest little maidens that mortal man had ever beheld. Their lovely hair was fine as a spider's web; their eyes were kind and smiling, their cheeks soft and dimpled, their mouths shapely as a cupid's bow and tinted like the petals of a rose. Upon their heads were set two crowns of fine spun gold, worked into fantastic shapes and set with glittering gems. Their robes were soft silks of pale yellow, with strings of sparkling emeralds for ornament.

Anything so lovely and fascinating as these little maids, who were precisely alike in every particular, neither Prince Marvel nor Nerle had ever dreamed could exist. They stood for a time spellbound and filled with admiration, while the two pairs of rulers bowed again and again before the dainty and lovable persons of their High Ki.

But it was hard for Nerle to keep quiet for long, and presently he exclaimed, in a voice loud enough to be heard by all present:

"By the Great Kika-koo of our friends the Ki, these darling High Ki of Twi are sweet enough to be kissed!"

Chapter 16 - The Rebellion of the High Ki

The bold speech of Nerle's made the two damsels laugh at the same time, and their sweet laughter sounded like rippling strains of harmonious music. But the two Ki-Ki frowned angrily, and the two Ki looked at the boy in surprise, as if wondering at his temerity.

"Who are these strangers?" asked the pretty High Ki, speaking together as all the twins of Twi did; "and why are they not mates, but only half of each other?"

"These questions, your Supreme Highnesses," said the blond-haired pair of Ki-Ki, "we are unable to answer."

"Perhaps, then, the strangers can answer themselves," said the little maids, smiling first upon the Ki-Ki and then upon the prisoners.

Prince Marvel bowed.

"I am from the great outside world," said he, "and my name is Prince Marvel. Until now I have never seen people that live in pairs, and speak in unison, and act in the same way and think the same thoughts. My world is much bigger than your world, and in it every person is proud to think and act for himself. You say I am only a 'half,' but that is not so. I am perfect, without a counterpart; my friend Nerle is perfect without a counterpart, and it is yourselves who are halved. For in the Land of

Twi no person is complete or perfect without its other half, and it seems to take two of you to make one man or one maid."

The sweet faces of the twin High Ki grew thoughtful at this speech, and they said:

"Indeed, it may be you are right. But it is our custom in Twi to do everything double and to live double." Then, turning to the Ki, they asked: "Why have you brought these strangers here?"

"To ask your Supreme Highnesses to permit them to return again to the world from whence they came," answered the Ki, both of them regarding their supreme rulers earnestly.

But here the Ki-Ki spoke up quickly in their mild voices, saying:

"That is not our idea, your Highnesses. We, the Ki-Ki of Twi, think it best the strangers should be put to death. And we pray your Supreme Highnesses to favor our wish."

The two little maids looked from the Ki to the Ki-Ki, and frowned and pouted their rosy lips in evident perplexity.

But Nerle whispered to Prince Marvel:

"It's all up with us! I know very well why her royal doublets always favors the Ki-Ki. It's because they are young and handsome, while the Ki are old and ugly. Both of her will condemn us to death, you see if she don't!"

This seemed somewhat mixed, but Nerle was in earnest, and Prince Marvel, who had not forgotten his fairy lore, began to weave a silent spell over the head of the nearest twin High Ki. But just as it was completed, and before he had time to work the spell on the other twin, the Ki-Ki grew impatient, and exclaimed:

"We beg your Highnesses not to keep us waiting. Let us have your decision at once!"

And the twin maidens raised their fair heads and replied. But the reply was of such a nature that both the old Ki and both the young Ki-Ki staggered backward in amazement. For one of the twin High Ki said:

"They shall die!"

And the other twin High Ki said at the same instant:

"They shall NOT die!"

Had twin thunderbolts fallen through the twin roofs of the twin palaces and struck the twin Ki and the twin Ki-Ki upon their twin heads it would have created no more stupendous a sensation than did this remark. Never before had any two halves of a twin of the Land of Twi thought differently or spoken differently. Indeed, it startled the two maidens themselves as much as it did their hearers, for each one turned her head toward the other and, for the first time in her life, looked into the other's face!

This act was fully as strange as their speech, and a sudden horrible thought came into the startled heads of the twin Ki and the twin Ki-Ki: THE HIGH KI OF TWI WAS NO LONGER ONE, BUT TWO. AND THESE TWO WERE THINKING AND ACTING EACH INDEPENDENT OF THE OTHER!

It is no wonder the shock rendered them speechless for a time, and they stood swaying their four bodies, with their eight eyes bulging out like those of fishes and their four mouths wide open, as if the two pairs had become one quartet.

The faces of the two maids flushed as they gazed upon each other.

"How DARE you contradict me?" asked one.

"How dare you contradict ME?" demanded the other, and not only were these questions asked separately, but the accent on the words was different. And their twin minds seemed to get farther apart every moment.

"I'm the High Ki of Twi!" said one.

"You're not! I'M the High Ki!" retorted the other.

"The strangers shall die!" snapped one.

"They shall live!" cried the other. "My will is supreme."

"It's not! MY will is supreme," returned the other twin.

The bald heads of the ancient Ki were bobbing in amazement, first to one maid and then toward the other. The blond hairs of the two Ki-Ki were standing almost on end, and their eyes stared straight before them as if stupefied with astonishment. Nerle was bellowing with rude laughter and holding his sides to keep from getting a stitch in them, while Prince Marvel stood quietly attentive and smiling with genuine amusement. For he alone understood what had happened to separate the twin High Ki.

The girls did not seem to know how to act under their altered conditions. After a time one of them said:

"We will leave our dispute to be settled by the Ki and the Ki-Ki."

"Very well," agreed the other.

"Then I say your half is right," declared the Ki-Ki, both their right forefingers pointing to the maiden who had condemned the strangers to death.

"And I decide that your half is right," exclaimed the Ki, both their trembling forefingers pointing to the maiden who had said the strangers should live.

"Well?" said one girl.

"Well?" said the other.

"The powers of the Ki and the Ki-Ki are equal," said the first. "We are no nearer a settlement of our dispute than we were before."

"My dear young ladies," said Prince Marvel, politely, "I beg you will take time to think the matter over, and see if you can not come to an agreement. We are in no hurry."

"Very well," decided the twins, speaking both together this time. "We command you all to remain in the palace until we have settled our own strange dispute. The servants will care for you, and when we are ready to announce our decision we shall again send for you."

Every one bowed at this command and retired from the room; but Nerle looked over his shoulder as he went through the doorway, and saw that the two High Ki had turned in their seats and were facing each other, and that both their faces wore angry and determined expressions.

Chapter 17 - The Separation of the High Ki

For nearly a week Prince Marvel and Nerle remained confined to the palace and gardens of the High Ki. Together with the twin Ki, who seemed to be friendly to them, they occupied one of the twin palaces, while the Ki-Ki secluded themselves in the other.

The pretty High Ki maidens they did not see at all, nor did they know what part of the palaces they occupied, not being permitted to wander away from the rooms allotted to them, except to walk in the garden. There was no way for them to escape, had they felt inclined to, for the silver steps had disappeared.

From the garden walks they sometimes caught sight of the solemn heads of the handsome Ki-Ki looking at them through the twin windows of the other palace, and although the expression of their faces was always mild and gentle, Nerle and Marvel well knew the Ki-Ki were only waiting in the hope of having them killed.

"Are you nervous about the decision of the pretty High Ki?" asked Nerle one day.

"No, indeed," said the prince, laughing; "for I do not expect them to kill me, in any event."

"If I felt as sure of my safety," returned the boy, "it would destroy all my pleasure. These are really happy days for me. Every moment I expect to see the executioner arrive with his ax."

"The executioner is double," said the two old Ki, breaking into the conversation. "You should say you expect to see the executioners arrive with their axes."

"Then how will they cut off my head with two axes? For I suppose they will both chop at the same time, and I have but one neck."

"Wait and see," answered the two Ki, sighing deeply and rubbing their red noses thoughtfully.

"Oh, I'll wait," answered the boy; "but as for seeing them cut off my head, I refuse; for I intend to shut my eyes."

So they sat in their rooms or walked in the gardens, yawning and waiting, until one day, just as the two clocks on the wall were striking twenty-four o'clock, the door opened and to their surprise one of the High Ki twins walked in upon them.

She was as sweet and fair to look upon as when she occupied one of the beautiful thrones, but at first no one could tell which of the High Ki she was their friend or their enemy. Even the Ki were puzzled and anxious, until the girl said:

"My other half and I have completely separated, for we have agreed to disagree for all time. And she has gone to ask the Ki-Ki to assist her, for war is declared between us. And hereafter her color is to be the green and mine the yellow, and we intend to fight until one of us conquers and overthrows the other."

This announcement was interesting to Marvel and Nerle, but greatly shocked the aged Ki, who asked:

"What is to become of our kingdom? Half of a High Ki can not rule it. It is against the law."

"I will make my own laws when I have won the fight," returned the girl, with a lovely smile; "so do not let that bother you. And now tell me, will you help me to fight my battles?"

"Willingly!" exclaimed Nerle and Prince Marvel, almost as if they had been twins of Twi. And the Ki rubbed their bald heads a moment, and then sneezed together and wiped their eyes on faded yellow handkerchiefs, and finally declared they would "stick to her Supreme Highness through thick and thin!"

"Then go over the wall to the cities, at once, and get together all the soldiers to fight for me and my cause," commanded the girl.

The twin Ki at once left the room, and the High Ki sat down and began to ask questions of Prince Marvel and Nerle about the big outside world from whence they came. Nerle was rather shy and bashful before the dainty little maiden, whose yellow robe contrasted delightfully with her pink cheeks and blue eyes and brown flowing locks; but Prince Marvel did not mind girls at all, so he talked with her freely, and she in return allowed him to examine the pretty gold crown she wore upon her brow.

By and by the Ki came back with both faces sad and gloomy.

"Your Highness," they announced, "we have bad news for you. The other High Ki, who is wearing a green gown, has been more prompt in action than yourself. She and the Ki-Ki have secured the silver steps and will allow no others to use them; and already they have sent for the soldiers of the royal armies to come and aid them. So we are unable to leave the garden, and presently the army will be here to destroy us."

Then the girl showed her good courage; for she laughed and said:

"Then we must remain here and fight to the last; and if I am unable to save you, who are my friends, it will be because I can not save myself."

This speech pleased Prince Marvel greatly. He kissed the little maid's hand respectfully and said:

"Fear nothing, your Highness. My friend and I are not so helpless as you think. We consider it our privilege to protect and save you, instead of your saving us; and we are really able to do this in spite of the other High Ki and her entire army."

So they remained quietly in the palace the rest of that day, and no one molested them in the least. In the evening the girl played and sang for them, and the ancient pair of Ki danced a double-shuffle for their amusement that nearly convulsed them with laughter. For one danced exactly like the other, and the old men's legs were still very nimble, although their wrinkled faces remained anxiously grave throughout their antics. Nerle also sang a song about the King of Thieves whom Prince Marvel had conquered, and another about the Red Rogue of Dawna, so that altogether the evening passed pleasantly enough, and they managed to forget all their uneasy doubts of the morrow.

When at last they separated for the night, Prince Marvel alone did not seek his bed; there was still some business he wished to transact. So he shut himself up in his room and summoned before him, by means of his fairy knowledge, the Prince of the Knooks, the King of the Ryls and the Governor of the Goblins. These were all three his especial friends, and he soon told them the story of the quarrel and separation of the twin High Ki, and claimed their assistance. Then he told them how they might aid him, and afterward dismissed them. Having thus accomplished his task, the fairy prince went to bed and slept peacefully the remainder of the night.

The next morning the blond Ki-Ki and all the army of Twi, which had been won to their cause, came climbing up the silver steps and over the wall to the palace of the green High Ki; but what was their amazement to find the twin palaces separated by a wall so high that no ladders nor steps they possessed could reach to the top! It had been built in a single night, and only Prince Marvel and his fairy friends knew how the work had been done so quickly.

The yellow High Ki, coming downstairs to breakfast with her friends, found herself securely shut in from her enemies, and the bald-headed old Ki were so pleased to escape that they danced another jig from pure joy.

Over the wall could be heard the shouts and threats of the army of Twi, who were seeking a way to get at the fugitives; but for the present our friends knew themselves to be perfectly safe, and they could afford to laugh at the fury of the entire population of Twi.

Chapter 18 - The Rescue of the High Ki

After several days of siege Prince Marvel began to feel less confident of the safety of his little party. The frantic Ki-Ki had built double battering-rams and were trying to batter down the high wall; and they had built several pairs of long ladders with which to climb over the wall; and their soldiers were digging two tunnels in the ground in order to crawl under the wall.

Not at once could they succeed, for the wall was strong and it would take long to batter it down; and Nerle stood on top of the wall and kicked over the ladders as fast as the soldiers of Twi set them up; and the gray-bearded Ki stood in the garden holding two big flat boards with which to whack the heads of any who might come through the tunnels.

But Prince Marvel realized that the perseverance of his foes might win in the end, unless he took measures to defeat them effectually. So he summoned swift messengers from among the Sound

Elves, who are accustomed to travel quickly, and they carried messages from him to Wul-Takim, the King of the Reformed Thieves, and to King Terribus of Spor, who had both promised him their assistance in case he needed it. The prince did not tell his friends of this action, but after the messengers had been dispatched he felt easier in his mind.

The little High Ki remained as sweet and brave and lovable as ever, striving constantly to cheer and encourage her little band of defenders. But none of them was very much worried, and Nerle confided to the maiden in yellow the fact that he expected to suffer quite agreeably when the Ki-Ki at last got him in their clutches.

Finally a day came when two big holes were battered through the wall, and then the twin soldiers of Twi poured through the holes and began to pound on the doors of the palace itself, in which Prince Marvel and Nerle, the Ki and the yellow High Ki had locked themselves as securely as possible.

The prince now decided it was high time for his friends to come to their rescue; but they did not appear, and before long the doors of the palace gave way and the soldiers rushed upon them in a vast throng.

Nerle wanted to fight, and to slay as many of the Twi people as possible; but the prince would not let him.

"These poor soldiers are but doing what they consider their duty," he said, "and it would be cruel to cut them down with our swords. Have patience, I pray you. Our triumph will come in good time."

The Ki-Ki, who came into the palace accompanied by the green High Ki, ordered the twin soldiers to bind all the prisoners with cords. So one pair of soldiers bound the Ki and another pair Nerle and the prince, using exactly the same motions in the operation. But when it came to binding the yellow High Ki the scene was very funny. For twin soldiers tried to do the binding, and there was only one to bind; so that one soldier went through the same motions as his twin on empty air, and when his other half had firmly bound the girl, his own rope fell harmless to the ground. But it seemed impossible for one of the twins to do anything different from the other, so that was the only way the act could be accomplished.

Then the green-robed High Ki walked up to the one in yellow and laughed in her face, saying:

"You now see which of us is the most powerful, and therefore the most worthy to rule. Had you remained faithful to our handsome Ki-Ki, as I did, you would not now be defeated and disgraced."

"There is no disgrace in losing one battle," returned the other girl, proudly. "You are mistaken if you think you have conquered me, and you are wrong to insult one who is, for the time being, your captive."

The maiden in green looked for an instant confused and ashamed; then she tossed her pretty head and walked away.

They led all the prisoners out into the garden and then through the broken wall, and up and down the silver steps, into the great square of the cities of Twi. And here all the population crowded around them, for this was the first time any of them had seen their High Ki, or even known that they were girls; and the news of their quarrel and separation had aroused a great deal of excitement.

"Let the executioners come forward!" cried the Ki-Ki, gleefully, and in answer to the command the twin executioners stepped up to the prisoners.

They were big men, these executioners, each having a squint in one eye and a scar on the left cheek. They polished their axes a moment on their coat-sleeves, and then said to Prince Marvel and Nerle, who were to be the first victims:

"Don't dodge, please, or our axes may not strike the right place. And do not be afraid, for the blows will only hurt you an instant. In the Land of Twi it is usually considered a pleasure to be executed by us, we are so exceedingly skillful." "I can well believe that," replied Nerle, although his teeth were chattering.

But at this instant a loud shout was heard, and the twin people of Twi all turned their heads to find themselves surrounded by throngs of fierce enemies.

Prince Marvel smiled, for he saw among the new-comers the giants and dwarfs and the stern Gray Men of King Terribus, with their monarch calmly directing their movements; and on the other side of the circle were the jolly faces and bushy whiskers of the fifty-nine reformed thieves, with burly Wul-Takim at their head.

Chapter 19 - The Reunion of the High Ki

The twins of Twi were too startled and amazed to offer to fight with the odd people surrounding them. Even the executioners allowed their axes to fall harmlessly to the ground, and the double people, soldiers and citizens alike, turned to stare at the strangers in wonder.

"We're here, Prince!" yelled Wul-Takim, his bristly beard showing over the heads of those who stood between.

"Thank you," answered Prince Marvel.

"And the men of Spor are here!" added King Terribus, who was mounted on a fine milk-white charger, richly caparisoned.

"I thank the men of Spor," returned Prince Marvel, graciously.

"Shall we cut your foes into small pieces, or would you prefer to hang them?" questioned the King of the Reformed Thieves, loudly enough to set most of his hearers shivering.

But now the little maid in yellow stepped up to Prince Marvel and, regarding the youthful knight with considerable awe, said sweetly:

"I beg you will pardon my people and spare them. They are usually good and loyal subjects, and if they fought against me, their lawful High Ki, it was only because they were misled by my separation from my other half."

"That is true," replied the prince; "and as you are still the lawful High Ki of Twi, I will leave you to deal with your own people as you see fit. For those who have conquered your people are but your own allies, and are still under your orders, as I am myself."

Hearing this, the green High Ki walked up to her twin High Ki and said, boldly:

"I am your prisoner. It is now your turn. Do with me as you will."

"I forgive you," replied her sister, in kindly tones.

Then the little maid who had met with defeat gave a sob and turned away weeping, for she had expected anything but forgiveness.

And now the Ki-Ki came forward and, bowing their handsome blond heads before the High Ki, demanded: "Are we forgiven also?"

"Yes," said the girl, "but you are no longer fit to be rulers of my people. Therefore, you are henceforth deprived of your honorable offices of Ki-Ki, which I shall now bestow upon these good captains here," and she indicated the good-natured officers who had first captured the prince and Nerle.

The people of Twi eagerly applauded this act, for the captains were more popular with them than the former Ki-Ki; but the blond ones both flushed with humiliation and anger, and said:

"The captains fought against you, even as we did."

"Yet the captains only obeyed your orders," returned the High Ki. "So I hold them blameless."

"And what is to become of us now?" asked the former Ki-Ki.

"You will belong to the common people, and earn your living playing tunes for them to dance by," answered the High Ki. And at this retort every one laughed, so that the handsome youths turned away with twin scowls upon their faces and departed amidst the jeers of the crowd.

"Better hang 'em to a tree, little one," shouted Wul-Takim, in his big voice; "they won't enjoy life much, anyhow."

But the maid shook her pretty head and turned to the prince.

"Will you stay here and help me to rule my kingdom?" she asked.

"I can not do that," replied Prince Marvel, "for I am but a wandering adventurer and must soon continue my travels. But I believe you will be able to rule your people without my help."

"It is not so easy a task," she answered, sighing. "For I am singular and my people are all double."

"Well, let us hold a meeting in your palace," said the prince, "and then we can decide what is best to be done."

So they dismissed the people, who cheered their High Ki enthusiastically, returning quietly to their daily tasks and the gossip that was sure to follow such important events as they had witnessed.

The army of King Terribus and the fifty-nine reformed thieves went to the twin palaces of the Ki and the Ki-Ki and made merry with feasting and songs to celebrate their conquest. And the High Ki, followed by the prince, Nerle, King Terribus and Wul-Takim, as well as by the Ki and the newly-appointed Ki-Ki, mounted the silver steps and passed over the wall to the royal palaces. The green High Ki followed them, still weeping disconsolately.

When they had all reached the throne-room, the High Ki seated herself on one of the beautiful thrones and said:

"By some strange chance, which I am unable to explain, my twin and I have become separated; so that instead of thinking and acting alike, we are now individuals, as are all the strange men who have passed through the hole in the hedge. And, being individuals, we can no longer agree, nor can one of us lawfully rule over the Kingdom of Twi, where all the subjects are twins, thinking and acting in unison."

Said Prince Marvel:

"Your Highness, I alone can explain why you became separated from your twin. By means of a fairy enchantment, which I learned years ago, I worked upon you a spell, which compelled your brain to work independent of your sister's brain. It seems to me that it is better each person should think her own thoughts and live her own life, rather than be yoked to another person and obliged to think and act as a twin, or one-half of a complete whole. And since you are now the one High Ki, and the acknowledged ruler of this country, I will agree to work the same fairy spell on all your people, so that no longer will there be twin minds in all this Land of Twi."

"But all the cows and dogs and horses and other animals are double, as well as the people," suggested the old Ki, blinking their little eyes in amazement at the thought of being forever separated from each other.

"I can also work the spell upon all the twin animals," said the prince, after a moment's hesitation.

"And all our houses are built double, with twin doors and windows and chimneys, to accommodate our twin people," continued the High Ki. "And the trees and flowers, and even the blades of grass, are all double. And our roads are double, and, and everything else is double. I alone, the ruler of this land, am singular!"

Prince Marvel became thoughtful now, for he did not know how to separate trees and flowers, and it would be a tedious task to separate the twin houses.

"Why not leave the country as it is?" asked King Terribus of Spor. "The High Ki is welcome to come to my castle to live, and then she need no longer bother about the Land of Twi, which seems to me a poor place, after all."

"And your sister may come with me to my cave, and be the queen of the reformed thieves, which is a much more important office than being High Ki of Twi," added big Wul-Takim, who had placed the maiden in green upon a cushion at his feet, and was striving to comfort her by gently stroking her silken hair with his rough hand.

"But I love my country, and do not wish to leave it," answered the yellow High Ki. "And I love my twin sister, and regret that our minds have become separated," she continued, sadly.

"I have it!" exclaimed Nerle. "Let the prince reunite you, making you regular twins of Twi again, and then you can continue to rule the country as the double High Ki, and everything will be as it was before."

The yellow High Ki clapped her pink hands with delight and looked eagerly at the prince.

"Will you?" she asked. "Will you please reunite us? And then all our troubles will be ended!"

This really seemed to Marvel the best thing to be done. So he led the maid in green to the other throne, where she had once sat, and after replacing the golden crown upon her brow he whispered a fairy spell of much mystical power.

Then the prince stepped back and regarded the maidens earnestly, and after a moment both the High Ki smiled upon him in unison and said, speaking the same words in the same voices and with the same accents:

"Thank you very much!"

Chapter 20 - Kwytoffle, the Tyrant

Having restored the High Ki to their former condition, to the great joy of the ancient Ki, Prince Marvel led his friends back to the palaces where his men were waiting.

They were just in time to prevent serious trouble, for the fifty-eight reformed thieves had been boasting of their prowess to the huge giants and tiny dwarfs of King Terribus, and this had resulted in a quarrel as to which were the best fighters. Had not their masters arrived at the right moment there would certainly have been a fierce battle and much bloodshed, and all over something of no importance.

Terribus and Wul-Takim soon restored order, and then they accompanied the Ki and the Ki-Ki to the public square, where the people were informed that their Supreme Highnesses, the High Ki, had been reunited and would thereafter rule them with twin minds as well as twin bodies. There was great rejoicing at this news, for every twin in Twi was glad to have his troubles ended so easily and satisfactorily.

That night the ryls and knooks and other invisible friends of Prince Marvel came and removed the dividing wall between the twin palaces of the High Ki, repairing speedily all the damage that had been done. And when our friends called upon the High Ki the next morning they found the two maids again dressed exactly alike in yellow robes, with strings of sparkling emeralds for ornament. And not even Prince Marvel could now tell one of the High Ki from the other.

As for the maids themselves, it seemed difficult to imagine they had ever existed apart for a single moment.

They were very pleasant and agreeable to their new friends, and when they heard that Prince Marvel was about to leave them to seek new adventures they said:

"Please take us with you! It seems to us that we ought to know something of the big outside world from whence you came. If we see other kingdoms and people we shall be better able to rule our own wisely."

"That seems reasonable," answered Marvel, "and I shall be very glad to have you accompany me. But who will rule the Land of Twi in your absence?"

"The Ki-Ki shall be the rulers," answered the High Ki, "and we will take the Ki with us."

"Then I will delay my departure until to-morrow morning," said the prince, "in order that your Highnesses may have time to prepare for the journey."

And then he went back to the palaces of the other rulers, where the Ki expressed themselves greatly pleased at the idea of traveling, and the new Ki-Ki were proud to learn they should rule for some time the Land of Twi.

Wul-Takim also begged to join the party, and so also did King Terribus, who had never before been outside of his own Kingdom of Spor; so Prince Marvel willingly consented.

The fifty-eight reformed thieves, led by Gunder, returned to their cave, where they were living comfortably on the treasure Prince Marvel had given them; and the Gray Men and giants and dwarfs of Spor departed for their own country.

In the morning Prince Marvel led his own gay cavalcade through the hole in the hedge, and they rode merrily away in search of adventure.

By his side were the High Ki, mounted upon twin chestnut ponies that had remarkably slender limbs and graceful, arched necks. The ponies moved with exactly the same steps, and shook their manes and swished their tails at exactly the same time. Behind the prince and the High Ki were King Terribus, riding his great white charger, and Wul-Takim on a stout horse of jet-black color. The two ancient Ki and Nerle, being of lesser rank than the others, brought up the rear.

"When we return to our Land of Twi," said the High Ki, "we shall close up for all time the hole you made in the hedge; for, if we are different from the rest of the world, it is better that we remain in seclusion."

"I think it is right you should do that," replied Prince Marvel. "Yet I do not regret that I cut a hole in your hedge."

"It was the hedge that delayed us in coming more promptly to your assistance," said Terribus; "for we had hard work to find the hole you had made, and so lost much valuable time."

"All is well that ends well!" laughed the prince. "You certainly came in good time to rescue us from our difficulties."

They turned into a path that led to Auriel, which Nerle had heard spoken of as "the Kingdom of the Setting Sun."

Soon the landscape grew very pleasant to look upon, the meadows being broad and green, with groups of handsome trees standing about. The twilight of the Land of Twi was now replaced by bright sunshine, and in the air was the freshness of the near-by sea.

At evening they came to a large farmhouse, where the owner welcomed them hospitably and gave them the best his house afforded.

In answer to their questions about the Kingdom of Auriel, he shook his head sadly and replied:

"It is a rich and beautiful country, but has fallen under great misfortunes. For when the good king died, about two years ago, the kingdom was seized by a fierce and cruel sorcerer, named Kwytoffle, who rules the people with great severity, and makes them bring him all their money and valuable possessions. So every one is now very poor and unhappy, and that is a great pity in a country so fair and fertile."

"But why do not the people rebel?" asked Nerle.

"They dare not rebel," answered the farmer, "because they fear the sorcery of Kwytoffle. If they do not obey him he threatens to change them into grasshoppers and June-bugs."

"Has he ever changed any one into a grasshopper or a June-bug?" asked Prince Marvel.

"No; but the people are too frightened to oppose him, and so he does not get the opportunity. And he has an army of fierce soldiers, who are accustomed to beat the people terribly if they do not carry every bit of their wealth to the sorcerer. So there is no choice but to obey him."

"We certainly ought to hang this wicked creature!" exclaimed Wul-Takim.

"I wish I had brought my Fool-Killer with me," sighed King Terribus; "for I could have kept him quite busy in this kingdom."

"Can not something be done to rescue these poor people from their sad fate?" asked the lovely High Ki, anxiously.

"We will make a call upon this Kwytoffle to-morrow," answered Prince Marvel, "and see what the fellow is like."

"Alas! Alas!" wailed the good farmer, "you will all become grasshoppers and June-bugs, every one of you!"

But none of the party seemed to fear that, and having passed the night comfortably with the farmer they left his house and journeyed on into the Kingdom of Auriel.

Before noon they came upon the edge of a forest, where a poor man was chopping logs into firewood. Seeing Prince Marvel's party approach, this man ran toward them waving his hands and shouting excitedly:

"Take the other path! Take the other path!"

"And why should we take the other path?" inquired the prince, reining in his steed.

"Because this one leads to the castle of the great sorcerer, Kwytoffle," answered the man.

"But there is where we wish to go," said Marvel.

"What! You wish to go there?" cried the man. "Then you will be robbed and enslaved!"

"Not as long as we are able to fight," laughed the big Wul-Takim.

"If you resist the sorcerer, you will be turned into grasshoppers and June-bugs," declared the man, staring at them in wonder.

"How do you know that?" asked Marvel.

"Kwytoffle says so. He promises to enchant every one who dares defy his power."

"Has any one ever yet dared defy him?" asked Nerle.

"Certainly not!" said the man. "No one wishes to become a June-bug or a grasshopper. No one dares defy him.".

"I am anxious to see this sorcerer," exclaimed King Terribus. "He ought to prove an interesting person, for he is able to accomplish his purposes by threats alone."

"Then let us ride on," said Marvel.

"Dear us! Dear us!" remonstrated the bald-headed Ki; "are we to become grasshoppers, then?"

"We shall see," returned the prince, briefly.

"With your long legs," added the pretty pair of High Ki, laughingly, "you ought to be able to jump farther than any other grasshopper in the kingdom."

"Great Kika-koo!" cried the Ki, nervously, "what a fate! what a terrible fate! And your Highnesses, I suppose, will become June-bugs, and flutter your wings with noises like buzz-saws!"

Chapter 21 - The Wonderful Book of Magic

Whatever their fears might be, none of Prince Marvel's party hesitated to follow him along the path through the forest in search of the sorcerer, and by and by they came upon a large clearing. In the middle of this open space was a big building in such bad repair that its walls were tumbling down in several places, and all around it the ground was uncared for and littered with rubbish. A man was walking up and down in front of this building, with his head bowed low; but when he heard the sound of approaching horses' hoofs he looked up and stared for a moment in amazement. Then, with a shout of rage, he rushed toward them and caught Prince Marvel's horse by the bridle.

"How dare you!" he cried; "how dare you enter my forest?"

Marvel jerked his bridle from the man's grasp and said in return:

"Who are you?"

"Me! Who am I? Why, I am the great and powerful Kwytoffle! So beware! Beware my sorcery!"

They all looked at the man curiously. He was short and very fat, and had a face like a puff-ball, with little red eyes and scarcely any nose at all. He wore a black gown with scarlet grasshoppers and june-bugs embroidered upon the cloth; and his hat was high and peaked, with an imitation grasshopper of extraordinary size perched upon its point. In his right hand he carried a small black wand, and around his neck hung a silver whistle on a silver cord.

Seeing that the strangers were gazing on him so earnestly, Kwytoffle thought they were frightened; so he said again, in a big voice:

"Beware my vengeance!"

"Beware yourself!" retorted the prince. "For if you do not treat us more respectfully, I shall have you flogged."

"What! Flog me!" shouted Kwytoffle, furiously. "For this I will turn every one of you into grasshoppers, unless you at once give me all the wealth you possess!"

"Poor man!" exclaimed Nerle; "I can see you are longing for that flogging. Will you have it now?" and he raised his riding-whip above his head.

Kwytoffle stumbled backward a few paces and blew shrilly upon his silver whistle. Instantly a number of soldiers came running from the building, others following quickly after them until fully a hundred rough-looking warriors, armed with swords and axes, had formed in battle array, facing the little party of Prince Marvel.

"Arrest these strangers!" commanded Kwytoffle, in a voice like a roar. "Capture them and bind them securely, and then I will change them all into grasshoppers!"

"All right," answered the captain of the soldiers; and then he turned to his men and shouted: "Forward, double-quick march!"

They came on with drawn swords; at first running, and then gradually dropping into a walk, as they beheld Nerle, Wul-Takim, King Terribus and Marvel standing quietly waiting to receive them, weapons in hand and ready for battle. A few paces off the soldiers hesitated and stopped altogether, and Kwytoffle yelled at the captain:

"Why don't you go on? Why don't you capture them? Why don't you fight them?"

"Why, they have drawn their swords!" responded the captain, reproachfully.

"Who cares?" roared the sorcerer.

"We care," said the captain, giving a shudder, as he looked upon the strangers. "Their swords are sharp, and some of us would get hurt."

"You're cowards!" shrieked the enraged Kwytoffle. "I'll turn you all into June-bugs!"

At this threat the soldiers dropped their swords and axes, and all fell upon their knees, trembling visibly and imploring their cruel master not to change them into june-bugs.

"Bah!" cried Nerle, scornfully; "why don't you fight? If we kill you, then you will escape being June-bugs."

"The fact is," said the captain, woefully, "we simply can't fight. For our swords are only tin, and our axes are made of wood, with silver-paper pasted over them."

"But why is that?" asked Wul-Takim, while all the party showed their surprise.

"Why, until now we have never had any need to fight," said the captain, "for every one has quickly surrendered to us or run away the moment we came near. But you people do not appear to be properly frightened, and now, alas! since you have drawn upon us the great sorcerer's anger, we shall all be transformed into June-bugs."

"Yes!" roared Kwytoffle, hopping up and down with anger, "you shall all be June-bugs, and these strangers I will transform into grasshoppers!"

"Very well," said Prince Marvel, quietly; "you can do it now."

"I will! I will!" cried the sorcerer.

"Then why don't you begin?" inquired the prince.

"Why don't I begin? Why, I haven't got the enchantments with me, that's why. Do you suppose we great magicians carry around enchantments in our pockets?" returned the other, in a milder tone.

"Where do you keep your enchantments?" asked the prince.

"They're in my dwelling," snapped Kwytoffle, taking off his hat and fanning his fat face with the brim.

"Then go and get them," said Marvel.

"Nonsense! If I went to get the enchantments you would all run away!" retorted the sorcerer.

"Not so!" protested Nerle, who was beginning to be amused. "My greatest longing in life is to become a grasshopper."

"Oh, yes! PLEASE let us be grasshoppers!" exclaimed the High Ki maids in the same breath.

"We want to hop! We want to hop! Please, PLEASE let us hop!" implored the bald-headed Ki, winking their left eyes at Wul-Takim.

"By all means let us become grasshoppers," said King Terribus, smiling; and Wul-Takim added:

"I'm sure your soldiers would enjoy being June-bugs, for then they wouldn't have to work. Isn't that so, boys?"

The bewildered soldiers looked at one another in perplexity, and the still more bewildered sorcerer gazed on the speakers with staring eyes and wide-open mouth.

"I insist," said Prince Marvel, "upon your turning us into grasshoppers and your soldiers into June-bugs, as you promised. If you do not, then I will flog you, as I promised."

"Very well," returned the sorcerer, with a desperate look upon his face; "I'll go and find the enchantment."

"And we'll go with you," remarked the prince, pleasantly.

So the entire party accompanied Kwytoffle into the house, where they entered a large room that was in a state of much disorder.

"Let me see," said the sorcerer, rubbing his ears, as if trying to think; "I wonder if I put them in this cupboard. You see," he explained, "no one has ever before dared me to transform him into a June-bug or grasshopper, so I have almost forgotten where I keep my book of enchantments. No, it's not in the cupboard," he continued, looking there; "but it surely must be in this chest."

It was not in the chest, either, and so the sorcerer continued to look in all sorts of queer places for his book of enchantments, without finding it. Whenever he paused in his search Prince Marvel would say, sternly:

"Go on! Find the book! Hunt it up. We are all anxious to become grasshoppers." And then Kwytoffle would set to work again, although big drops of perspiration were now streaming down his face.

Finally he pulled an old book from underneath the pillow of his bed, and crying, "Here it is!" carried it to the window.

He turned a few leaves of the book and then said:

"How unfortunate! The compound I require to change you into grasshoppers must be mixed on the first day of September; and as this is now the eighth day of September I must wait nearly a year before I can work the enchantment."

"How about the June-bugs?" asked Nerle.

"Oh! Ah!. The June-bug mixture can only be made at the dark o' the moon," said the sorcerer, pretending to read, "and that is three weeks from now."

"Let me read it," said Prince Marvel, suddenly snatching the book from Kwytoffle's hands. Then he turned to the title-page and read:

"'Lives of Famous Thieves and Impostors.' Why, this is not a book of enchantments."

"That is what I suspected," said Terribus.

"No one but a sorcerer can read the enchantments in this book," declared Kwytoffle; but he hung his head with a sheepish look, for he knew his deception had been well understood.

"Is your own history written in this volume?" inquired Marvel.

"No," answered the sorcerer.

"Then it ought to be," said the prince, "for you are no sorcerer at all, but merely a thief and an impostor!"

Chapter 22 - The Queen of Plenta

The soldiers of Kwytoffle wanted to hang their old master at once, for he had won their enmity by abusing them in many ways; but Prince Marvel would not let them do this. However, they tied the false sorcerer to a post, and the captain gave him a good whipping, one lash for each letter in the words "grasshopper" and "June-bug." Kwytoffle howled loudly for mercy, but no one was at all sorry for him.

Wul-Takim tied a rope around the impostor's neck, and when the party left the castle they journeyed all through the kingdom of Auriel, and at every town or city they came to the reformed thief would cry out to the populace:

"Here is the terrible sorcerer Kwytoffle, who threatened to change you into grasshoppers and june-bugs. But you may see that he is a very common man, with no powers of sorcery whatever!"

And then the people would laugh and pelt mud at their former tyrant, and thank Prince Marvel for having exposed the false and wicked creature.

And they called the son of their old king back to his lawful throne, where he ruled wisely and well; and the hoarded wealth of Kwytoffle was divided among the people again, and soon the country became prosperous once more.

This adventure was very amusing to the pretty High Ki of Twi. It afforded them laughter for many days, and none of the party ever saw a grasshopper or a june-bug afterward without thinking of the terrible sorcerer Kwytoffle.

They left that disgraced person grooming horses for his board in the stables of the new king, and proceeded upon their journey.

Without further event they reached the splendid southern Kingdom of Plenta, which was the most delightfully situated of any dominion in the Enchanted Island of Yew. It was ruled by a good and generous queen, who welcomed the strangers to her palace and gave a series of gay entertainments in their honor.

King Terribus was especially an object of interest, for every one had heard his name and feared him and his fierce people. But when they beheld his pleasant countenance and listened to his gentle voice they began to regard him with much love and respect; and really Terribus was worthy of their friendship since he had changed from a deformed monster into an ordinary man, and had forbidden his people ever again to rob and plunder their weaker neighbors.

But the most popular personages visiting at the court of the Queen of Plenta were the lovely High Ki of Twi. Although beautiful girls abounded in this kingdom, none could compare with the royal twins, and their peculiar condition only served to render them the more interesting.

Two youths would approach the High Ki at the same time and invite them to dance, and in united voices they would accept the invitation and go whirling around the room with exactly the same steps, laughing at the same instant and enjoying the dance equally. But if one youth asked his partner a question, both the twins would make answer, and that was sure to confuse and embarrass the youth. Still, the maids managed very well to adapt themselves to the ways of people who were singular, although they sometimes became a little homesick for Twi, where they were like all the other people.

The bald-headed Ki kept watchful eyes on their youthful rulers, and served them very cheerfully. But with all their travels and experiences, the old men could never be convinced it was better to be singular than double.

Prince Marvel was the real hero of the party, and Nerle received much attention on account of his master's popularity. He did not seem as unhappy as usual, and when the prince inquired the reason, his esquire answered that he believed the excitement of their adventures was fast curing him of his longing for something he could not have. As for the pleasure of suffering, he had had some experience of that, too, and it was not nearly so delightful as he had expected.

Wul-Takim was not a society man, so he stayed around the royal stables and made friends with the grooms, and traded his big black horse for two bay ones and a gold neck-chain, and was fairly content with his lot.

And so the party enjoyed several happy weeks at the court of the good Queen of Plenta, until one day the terrible news arrived that carried them once more into exciting adventures.

Chapter 23 - The Red Rogue of Dawna

One morning, while they were all standing in the courtyard waiting for their horses, as they were about to go for a ride, a courier came galloping swiftly up to the palace and cried:

"Does any one know where Prince Marvel can be found?"

"I am Prince Marvel," replied the young knight, stepping out from among the others.

"Then have I reached my journey's end!" said the courier, whose horse was nearly exhausted from long and hard riding. "The Lady Seseley is in great danger, and sends for you to come and rescue her. The great Baron Merd, her father, has been killed and his castle destroyed, and all his people are either captives or have been slain outright."

"And who has done this evil thing?" asked Prince Marvel, looking very stern and grave.

"The Red Rogue of Dawna," answered the messenger. "He quarreled with the Baron Merd and sent his savage hordes to tear down his castle and slay him. I myself barely escaped with my life, and the Lady Seseley had but time to say, before she was carried off, that if I could find Prince Marvel he would surely rescue her."

"And so I will!" declared the prince, "if she be still alive."

"Who is this Lady Seseley?" asked Nerle, who had come to his master's side.

"She is my first friend, to whom I owe my very existence. It is her image, together with those of her two friends, which is graven on my shield," answered Prince Marvel, thoughtfully.

"And what will you do?" inquired the esquire.

"I must go to her at once."

When they heard of his mission all the party insisted on accompanying him. Even the dainty High Ki could not be deterred by any thoughts of dangers they might encounter; and after some discussion Prince Marvel allowed them to join him.

So Wul-Takim sharpened his big broadsword, and Nerle carefully prepared his master's horse, so that before an hour had passed they were galloping toward the province of the Red Rogue of Dawna.

Prince Marvel knew little concerning this personage, but Nerle had much to tell of him. The Red Rogue had once been page to a wise scholar and magician, who lived in a fine old castle in Dawna and ruled over a large territory. The boy was very small and weak, smaller even than the average dwarf, and his master did not think it worth while to watch him. But one evening, while the magician was standing upon the top of the highest tower of his castle, the boy gave him a push from behind, and he met death on the sharp rocks below. Then the boy took his master's book of magic and found a recipe to make one grow. He made the mixture and swallowed it, and straightway began to grow big and tall. This greatly delighted him, until he found he was getting much bigger than the average man and rapidly becoming a giant. So he sought for a way to arrest the action of the magical draft; but before he could find it he had grown to enormous proportions, and was bigger than the biggest giant. There was nothing in the book of magic to make one grow smaller, so he was obliged to remain as he was, the largest man in the Enchanted Island.

All this had happened in a single night. The morning after his master's murder the page announced himself lord of the castle; and, seeing his enormous size, none dared deny his right to rule. On account of his bushy hair, which was fiery red in color, and the bushy red beard that covered his face when he became older, people came to call him the Red One. And after his evil deeds and quarrelsome temper had made him infamous throughout the island, people began to call him the Red Rogue of Dawna.

He had gathered around him a number of savage barbarians, as wicked and quarrelsome as himself, and so none dared to interfere with him, or even to meet him, if it were possible to avoid it.

This same Red Rogue it was who had drawn the good Baron Merd into a quarrel and afterward slain the old knight and his followers, destroyed his castle, and carried his little daughter Seseley and her girl friends, Berna and Helda, into captivity, shutting them up in his own gloomy castle.

The Red Rogue thought he had done a very clever thing, and had no fear of the consequences until one of his men came running up to the castle to announce that Prince Marvel and his companions were approaching to rescue the Lady Seseley.

"How many of them are there?" demanded the Red Rogue.

"There are eight, altogether," answered the man, "but two of them are girls."

"And they expect to force me to give up my captives?" asked the Red One, laughing with a noise like the roar of a waterfall. "Why, I shall make prisoners of every one of them!"

The man looked at his master fearfully, and replied:

"This Prince Marvel is very famous, and all people speak of his bravery and power. It was he who conquered King Terribus of Spor, and that mighty ruler is now his friend, and is one of the eight who approach."

The Red Rogue stopped laughing, for the fame of Spor's terrible king had long ago reached him. And he reflected that any one who could conquer the army of giants and dwarfs and Gray Men that served Terribus must surely be one to be regarded seriously. Moreover, and this was a secret, the Red Rogue had never been able to gain the strength to correspond with his gigantic size, but had ever remained as weak as when he was a puny boy. So he was accustomed to rely on his cunning and on the terror his very presence usually excited to triumph over his enemies. And he began to be afraid of this prince.

"You say two of the party are girls?" he asked.

"Yes," said the man, "but also among them are King Terribus himself, and the renowned Wul-Takim, formerly king of thieves, who was conquered by the prince, although accounted a hard fighter, and is now his devoted servant. And there are two old men who are just alike and have a very fierce look about them. They are said to come from the hidden Kingdom of Twi."

By this time the Red Rogue was thoroughly frightened, but he did not yet despair of defeating his enemies. He knew better than to attempt to oppose Prince Marvel by force, but he still hoped to conquer him by trickery and deceit.

Among the wonderful things that the Red Rogue's former master, the wise scholar and magician, had made were two large enchanted mirrors, which were set on each side of the great hallway of the castle. Heavy curtains were drawn over the surfaces of these mirrors, because they both possessed a dreadful magical power. For whenever any one looked into one of them his reflection was instantly caught and imprisoned in the mirror, and his body at the same time became invisible to all earthly eyes, only the mirror retaining his form.

While considering a way to prevent the prince from freeing the Lady Seseley, the Red Rogue happened to think of these mirrors, which had never yet been used. So he went stealthily into the great hall and drew aside the covering from one of the mirrors. He did not dare look into the mirror himself, but hurried away to another room, and then sent a page up a back stairway to summon the Lady Seseley and her two maids into his presence.

The girls at once obeyed, for they greatly feared the Red Rogue; and of course they descended the front stairway and walked through the great hall. At once the large mirror that had been exposed to view caught the eye of Seseley, and she paused to regard her reflection in the glass. Her two companions did likewise, and instantly all three girls became invisible, while the mirror held their reflections fast in its magic surface.

The Red Rogue was watching them through a crack in the door, and seeing the girls disappear he gave a joyful laugh and exclaimed:

"Now let Prince Marvel find them if he can!"

The three girls began to wander aimlessly through the castle; for not only were they invisible to others, but also to themselves and to one another, and they knew not what to do nor which way to turn.

Chapter 24 - The Enchanted Mirrors

Presently Prince Marvel and his party arrived and paused before the doors of the castle, where the Red Rogue stood bowing to them with mock politeness and with an evil grin showing on his red face.

"I come to demand the release of the Lady Seseley and her companions!" Prince Marvel announced, in a bold voice. "And I also intend to call you to account for the murder of Baron Merd."

"You must be at the wrong castle," answered the Red One, "for I have murdered no baron, nor have I any Lady Seseley as prisoner."

"Are you not the Red Rogue of Dawna?" demanded the prince.

"Men call me by that name," acknowledged the other.

"Then you are deceiving me," said the prince.

"No, indeed!" answered the Red Rogue, mockingly. "I wouldn't deceive any one for the world. But, if you don't believe me, you are welcome to search my castle."

"That I shall do," returned the prince, sternly, "whether I have your permission or not," and he began to dismount. But Nerle restrained him, saying:

"Master, I beg you will allow me to search the castle. For this Red Rogue is playing some trick upon us, I am sure, and if anything happened to you there would be no one to protect the little High Ki and our other friends."

"But suppose something should happen to you?" inquired the prince, anxiously.

"In that case," said Nerle, "you can avenge me."

The advice was so reasonable, under the circumstances, that the prince decided to act upon it.

"Very well," said he, "go and search the castle, and I will remain with our friends. But if anything happens to you, I shall call the Red Rogue to account."

So Nerle entered the castle, passing by the huge form of its owner, who only nodded to the boy and grinned with delight.

The esquire found himself in the great hall and began to look around him, but without seeing any one. Then he advanced a few steps and, to his surprise, discovered a large mirror, in which were reflected the faces and forms of three girls, as well as his own.

"Why, here they are!" he attempted to say; but he could not hear his own voice. He glanced down at himself but could see nothing at all, for his body had become invisible. His reflection was still in the glass, and he knew that his body existed the same as before; but although he yet saw plainly the hall and all that it contained, he could see neither himself nor any other person of flesh.

After waiting a considerable time for his esquire to reappear Prince Marvel became impatient.

"What have you done with Nerle?" he asked of the Red Rogue.

"Nothing," was the reply. "I have been here, plainly within your sight, every moment."

"Let me go and find him!" exclaimed King Terribus, and rushed into the castle before the prince could reply. But Terribus also encountered the enchanted mirror, and the prince waited in vain for his return.

Then Wul-Takim volunteered to go in search of the others, and drew his big, sharp sword before entering the hall. But an hour passed by and he did not return.

The Red Rogue was overjoyed at the success of his stratagem, and could scarce refrain from laughing outright at the prince's anxiety.

Marvel was really perplexed. He knew some treachery was afoot, but could not imagine what it was. And when the pretty High Ki declared their intention of entering the castle, he used every endeavor to dissuade them. But the twin girls would not be denied, so great was their curiosity. So the prince said:

"Well, we will all go together, so that the Ki and I may be able to protect you."

The Red Rogue gladly granted them admittance, and they passed him and entered the great hall.

The place appeared to them to be completely empty, so they walked along and came opposite the mirror. Here all stopped at once, and the twin High Ki uttered exclamations of surprise, and the twin Ki shouted, "Great Kika-koo!"

For there in the glass were the reflections of the three girls and Nerle and King Terribus and Wul-Takim. And there were also the reflections of the twin High Ki and the twin Ki. Only Prince Marvel's reflection was missing, and this was because of his fairy origin. For the glass could reflect and hold only the forms of mortals.

But the prince saw the reflections of all the others, and then made the discovery that the forms of the Ki and the High Ki had become invisible. No one except himself appeared to be standing in the great hall of the Red Rogue's castle! Yet grouped within the glass were the likenesses of all his friends, as well as those of Lady Seseley and her companions; and all were staring back at him earnestly, as if imploring him to save them.

The mystery was now explained, and Prince Marvel rushed from the hall to find the treacherous Red Rogue. But that clever trickster had hidden himself in an upper room, and for the present was safely concealed.

For a time Prince Marvel could not think what to do. Such magic was all unknown to him, and how to free the imprisoned forms of his friends was a real problem. He walked around the castle, but no one was in sight, the Rogue having given orders to all his people to keep away. Only the tethered horses did he see, and these raised their heads and whinnied as if in sympathy with his perplexity.

Then he went back into the hall and searched all the rooms of the castle without finding a single person. On his return he stopped in front of the mirror and sorrowfully regarded the faces of his friends, who again seemed to plead for relief.

And while he looked a sudden fit of anger came over him at being outwitted by this Red Rogue of Dawna. Scarcely knowing what he did, he seized his sword by the blade and struck the mirror a powerful blow with the heavy hilt. It shattered into a thousand fragments, which fell clattering upon the stone floor in every direction. And at once the charm was broken; each of his friends now became visible. They appeared running toward him from all parts of the castle, where they had been wandering in their invisible forms.

They called out joyful greetings to one another, and then all of them surrounded the prince and thanked him earnestly for releasing them.

The little Lady Seseley and her friends, Berna and Helda, were a bit shy in the presence of so many strangers; but they alone knew the prince's secret, and that he was a fairy transformed for a year; so they regarded him as an old and intimate acquaintance, and after being introduced by him to the others of his party they became more at ease.

The sweet little High Ki maids at once attracted Seseley, and she loved them almost at first sight. But it was Nerle who became the little lady's staunchest friend; for there was something rather mystical and unnatural to him about the High Ki, who seemed almost like fairies, while in Seseley he recognized a hearty, substantial girl of his own rank in life.

While they stood talking and congratulating one another outside of the castle, the Red Rogue of Dawna appeared among them. He had heard the noise of the smashing of his great mirror, and had come running downstairs from his hiding-place to find his cunning had all been for naught and his captives were free.

A furious anger then took possession of the Rogue, and forgetting his personal weakness he caught up a huge battle-ax and rushed out to hurl himself upon Prince Marvel, intending to do him serious injury.

But the prince was not taken unawares. He saw the Red Rogue coming and met him with drawn sword, striking quickly at the arm that wielded the big ax. The stroke was as sure as it was quick, and piercing the arm of the giant caused him to drop the ax with a howl of pain.

Then Prince Marvel seized the Red Rogue by the ear, which he was just tall enough to reach, and dragged him up the steps and into the castle, the big fellow crying for mercy at every step and trembling like a leaf through cowardice.

But down the hall Marvel marched him, seeking some room where the Rogue might be safely locked in. The great curtain that covered the second enchanted mirror now caught Prince Marvel's eye, and, still holding his prisoner by the ear, he reached out his left hand and pulled aside the drapery.

The Red Rogue looked to see what his captor was doing, and beheld his own reflection in the magic mirror. Instantly he gave a wild cry and disappeared, his body becoming absolutely invisible, while his coarse red countenance stared back from the mirror.

And then Prince Marvel gave a sigh of relief and dropped the curtain over the surface of the mirror. For he realized that the Red Rogue of Dawna had at last met with just punishment and was safely imprisoned for all time.

Chapter 25 - The Adventurers Separate

When Prince Marvel and his friends had ridden away from the castle the savage followers of the Red One came creeping up to listen for their master's voice. But silence reigned in every part of the castle, and after stealing fearfully through the rooms without seeing any one the fellows became filled with terror and fled from the place, never to return.

And afterward the neighbors whispered that the castle was haunted by the spirit of the terrible Red Rogue, and travelers dared not stop in the neighborhood, but passed by quickly and with averted faces.

The prince and his party rode gaily along toward the Kingdom of Heg, for Nerle had invited them all to visit his father's castle. They were very happy over their escape, and only the little Lady Seseley became sad at times, when she thought of her father's sad fate.

The Baron Neggar, who was Nerle's father, was not only a wealthy nobleman, but exceedingly kind and courteous; so that every member of Prince Marvel's party was welcomed to the big castle in a very hospitable manner.

Nerle was eagerly embraced by both his father and mother, who were overjoyed to see him return safe and sound after his wanderings and adventures.

"And have you been cured of your longing for something that you can not have?" asked the baron, anxiously.

"Not quite," said Nerle, laughing; "but I am more reconciled to my lot. For I find wherever I go people are longing for just the things they can not get, and probably would not want if they had them. So, as it seems to be the fate of most mortals to live unsatisfied, I shall try hereafter to be more contented."

These words delighted the good baron, and he gave a rich and magnificent feast in honor of his son's return.

The High Ki of Twi, after passing several pleasant days at Nerle's home, now decided that they had seen enough of the world and would be glad to return to their own kingdom, where all was peaceful and uneventful, and rule it to the end of their days. So the baron furnished them an escort of twenty men-at-arms, and these conducted the High Ki and the aged Ki safely back to the hole in the hedge.

And after they had entered the Land of Twi, the first act of the High Ki was to order the hedge repaired and the hole blocked up; and I have never heard that any one, from that time forth, ever succeeded in gaining admittance to the hidden kingdom. So its subsequent history is unknown.

King Terribus also bade the prince an affectionate farewell and rode back to his own kingdom; and burly Wul-Takim accompanied him as far as the cave, where the fifty-eight reformed thieves awaited him.

Nerle's mother gladly adopted the Lady Seseley and her two companions, and thereafter they made their home at the baron's castle. And years afterward, when they had grown to be women, Seseley was married to Nerle and became the lady of the castle herself.

Prince Marvel enjoyed the feasting and dancing at the castle very much, but after the party began to break up, and the High Ki and the Ki had left him, as well as King Terribus and honest Wul-Takim, the young knight grew thoughtful and sometimes uneasy, and his happy laugh was less frequently heard. Nerle often regarded his young master with a feeling of awe, for there occasionally came a look into Marvel's eyes that reminded him more of the immortals than of any human being. But the prince treated him with rare kindness and always pressed Nerle's hand affectionately when he bade him good night, for he had grown fond of his esquire. Also they had long conversations together, during which Nerle gleaned a great deal of knowledge and received some advice that was of much use to him in his later life.

One day Prince Marvel sought out Lady Seseley and said:

"Will you ride with me to the Forest of Lurla?"

"Willingly," she answered; and calling Berna and Helda to attend them, they mounted their horses and rode swiftly away, for it was a long distance to Lurla.

By noon the party entered the forest, and although the path they traversed was unknown to the girls, who had usually entered the forest from its other side, near to where the Baron Merd's castle had stood, the prince seemed to have no difficulty in finding his way.

He guided them carefully along the paths, his handsome war-charger stepping with much grace and dignity, until at length they came to a clearing.

Here the prince paused abruptly, and Seseley looked around her and at once recognized the place.

"Why," she exclaimed, in surprise, "it is the Fairy Bower!"

And then she turned to Prince Marvel and asked in a soft voice:

"Is the year ended, Prince?"

His smile was a bit sad as he answered, slowly:

"The year will be ended in five minutes!"

Chapter 26 - The End of the Year

The girls sat upon the green moss and waited. Prince Marvel stood silent beside his horse. The silver armor was as bright as the day he donned it, nor was there a dent in his untarnished shield.

The sword that had done such good service he held lightly in his hand, and the horse now and then neighed softly and turned to look at him with affectionate eyes.

Seseley began to tremble with excitement, and Berna and Helda stared at the prince with big round eyes.

But, after all, they saw nothing so remarkable as they expected. For Presently, and it all happened in a flash, Prince Marvel was gone from their midst, and a handsome, slender-limbed deer darted from the bower and was quickly lost in the thick forest. On the ground lay a sheet of bark and a twig from a tree, and beside them was Lady Seseley's white velvet cloak.

Then the three girls each drew a long breath and looked into one another's eyes, and, while thus engaged, a peal of silvery laughter sounded in their ears and made them spring quickly to their feet.

Before them stood a tiny and very beautiful fairy, clothed in floating gossamer robes of rose and pearl color, and with eyes sparkling like twin stars.

"Prince Marvel!" exclaimed the three, together.

"No, indeed!" cried the fairy, with a pretty little pout. "I am no one but myself; and, really, I believe I shall now be content to exist for a few hundred years in my natural form. I have quite enjoyed my year as a mortal; but after all there are, I find, some advantages in being a fairy. Good by, my dears!"

And with another ripple of laughter the pretty creature vanished, and the girls were left alone.

Chapter 27 - A Hundred Years Afterward

About a hundred years after Prince Marvel enjoyed his strange adventures in the Enchanted Island of Yew an odd thing happened.

A hidden mirror in a crumbling old castle of Dawna broke loose from its fastenings and fell crashing on the stone pavement of the deserted hall. And from amid the ruins rose the gigantic form of a man. His hair and beard were a fiery red, and he gazed at the desolation around him in absolute amazement.

It was the Red Rogue of Dawna, set free from his imprisonment.

He wandered out and found strange scenes confronting him, for during the hundred years a great change had taken place in the Enchanted Island. Great cities had been built and great kingdoms established. Civilization had won the people, and they no longer robbed or fought or indulged in magical arts, but were busily employed and leading respectable lives.

When the Red Rogue tried to tell folks who he was, they but laughed at him, thinking the fellow crazy. He tried to get together a band of thieves, as Wul-Takim had done in the old days, but none would join him.

And so, forced to be honest against his will, the Rogue was driven to earn a living by digging in the garden of a wealthy noble, of whom he had never before heard.

But often he would pause in his labors and lean on his spade, while thoughts of the old days of wild adventure passed through his mind in rapid succession; and then the big man would shake his red head with a puzzled air and mutter:

"I wonder who that Prince Marvel could have been! And I wonder what ever became of him!"

L Frank Baum - A Short Biography

Lyman Frank Baum was born on May 15, 1856 in Chittenango, New York. A sickly child he was schooled at home until the age of 12 when he was then sent to at Peekskill Military Academy. His parents may have thought he needed toughening up but two miserable years at the military academy saw him return home.

He was fascinated by printing and early on was given a printing press from which he produced a number of journals.

By age 20 he managed to combine his love of printing with that of poultry breeding, in particular a variety called The Hamburg, to produce the The Poultry Record, (In 1886, when Baum was 30 years old, his first book was published: The Book of the Hamburgs: A Brief Treatise upon the Mating, Rearing, and Management of the Different Varieties of Hamburgs).

He also had a life time infatuation with the Theatre which at times would bring him to near bankruptcy.

In 1880, his father built him a theatre in Richburg, New York, and Baum set about writing plays and gathering together an actor's company. The Maid of Arran, was his first, a melodrama with songs based on William Black's novel A Princess of Thule, proved a modest success. Baum not only wrote the play but composed songs for it (making it a prototypical musical, as its songs relate to the narrative), and acted in the leading role.

On November 9, 1882, Baum married Maud Gage, a daughter of Matilda Joslyn Gage, a famous women's suffrage and radical feminist activist. While Baum was touring with The Maid of Arran, the theatre in Richburg caught fire during a production of Baum's ironically-titled parlor drama, Matches, destroying not only the theatre, but the only known copies of many of Baum's scripts, including Matches, as well as costumes.

In July 1888, Baum and his wife moved to Aberdeen, Dakota Territory, where he opened a store, "Baum's Bazaar". His habit of giving out wares on credit led to the eventual bankrupting of the store, so he turned to editing a local newspaper; The Aberdeen Saturday Pioneer, where he also wrote a column, Our Landlady. In December 1890, Baum urged the wholesale extermination of all America's native peoples in a column he wrote on December 20, 1890, nine days before the Wounded Knee Massacre.

Whilst such views may have been fairly common then they seem all the more shocking in the context of his popular children's stories.

Baum's description of Kansas in The Wonderful Wizard of Oz is based on his experiences in drought-ridden South Dakota. While Baum was in South Dakota, he sang in a quartet that included a man who would become one of the first Populist Senators in the U.S., James Kyle.

After Baum's newspaper failed in 1891, he, Maud and their four sons moved to Humboldt Park, Chicago, where Baum took a job with the Evening Post. In 1897, and for several years thereafter he edited a magazine for advertising agencies focused on window displays in stores. The major department stores created elaborate Christmas time fantasies, using clockwork mechanisms that made people and animals appear to move.

In 1897, he wrote and published Mother Goose in Prose, a collection of Mother Goose rhymes written as prose stories, and illustrated by Maxfield Parrish. Mother Goose was a moderate success, and allowed Baum to quit his door-to-door sales job. In 1899 Baum partnered with illustrator W. W. Denslow, to publish Father Goose, His Book, a collection of nonsense poetry. The book was a success, becoming the best-selling children's book of the year.

In 1900, Baum and Denslow published The Wonderful Wizard of Oz to critical acclaim and financial success. It was the best-selling children's book for two years running. Baum went on to write thirteen more novels based on the places and people of the Land of Oz.

His writing was prolific though at times weak and he constantly delved into other challenges. In the 1900's he moved to the newly emerging film center of Hollywood and he began his own film company, he also planned and announced an amusement park of the California coast. He was a man rich in ideas and energy but many were ill thought out and ill fated. Still his fame was set as a beloved writer of children's fiction and the magnificence of the creation he called Oz.

On May 5, 1919, Baum suffered from a stroke. He died quietly the next day, nine days short of his 63rd birthday. At the end he mumbled in his sleep, "Now we can cross the Shifting Sands."

He was buried in Glendale's Forest Lawn Memorial Park Cemetery. His final Oz book, Glinda of Oz, was published on July 10, 1920.

The Oz series was continued long after his death by other authors, notably Ruth Plumly Thompson, who wrote an additional nineteen Oz books.

L Frank Baum - A Concise Bibliography

Oz Books
The Wonderful Wizard of Oz (1900)
The Marvelous Land of Oz (1904)
Queer Visitors from the Marvelous Land of Oz (1905, comic strip depicting 27 stories)
The Woggle-Bug Book (1905)
Ozma of Oz (1907)
Dorothy and the Wizard in Oz (1908)
The Road to Oz (1909)
The Emerald City of Oz (1910)
The Patchwork Girl of Oz (1913)
Little Wizard Stories of Oz (1913, collection of 6 short stories)
Tik-Tok of Oz (1914)

The Scarecrow of Oz (1915)
Rinkitink in Oz (1916)
The Lost Princess of Oz (1917)
The Tin Woodman of Oz (1918)
The Magic of Oz (1919, posthumously published)
Glinda of Oz (1920, posthumously published)
The Royal Book of Oz (1921, posthumous attribution—entirely the work of Ruth Plumly Thompson)

Non-Oz Books

Princess Truella, a character from The Magical Monarch of Mo, illustrated by Frank Ver Beck
Mother Goose in Prose (prose retellings of Mother Goose rhymes, (1897)
By the Candelabra's Glare (poetry, 1898)[52]
Father Goose: His Book (nonsense poetry, 1899)
The Magical Monarch of Mo (Originally published in 1900 as A New Wonderland) (fantasy, 1903)
The Army Alphabet (poetry, 1900)
The Navy Alphabet (poetry, 1900)
Dot and Tot of Merryland (fantasy, 1901)
American Fairy Tales (fantasy, 1901)
The Master Key: An Electrical Fairy Tale (fantasy, 1901)
The Life and Adventures of Santa Claus (fantasy, 1902)
The Enchanted Island of Yew (fantasy, 1903)
Queen Zixi of Ix (fantasy, 1905)
John Dough and the Cherub (fantasy, 1906)
Father Goose's Year Book: Quaint Quacks and Feathered Shafts for Mature Children, 1907)
The Daring Twins: A Story for Young Folk (novel, 1911)
The Sea Fairies (fantasy, 1911)
Sky Island (fantasy, 1912)
Phoebe Daring: A Story for Young Folk (novel, 1912!)
Our Married Life (novel, 1912)
Johnson (novel, 1912)
The Mystery of Bonita (novel, 1914)
Molly Oodle (novel, 1915)
Animal Fairy Tales (fantasy, 1905 as a magazine series)

Short Stories

This list omits stories that appeared in Our Landlady, American Fairy Tales, Animal Fairy Tales, Little Wizard Stories of Oz, and Queer Visitors from the Marvelous Land of Oz.

"They Played a New Hamlet" (April 28, 1895)
"A Cold Day on the Railroad" (May 26, 1895)
"Who Called 'Perry?'" (January 19, 1896)
"Yesterday at the Exhibition" (February 2, 1896)
"My Ruby Wedding Ring" (October 12, 1896)
"The Man with the Red Shirt" (c.1897, told to Matilda Jewell Gage, who wrote it down in 1905)
"How Scroggs Won the Reward" (May 5, 1897)
"The Extravagance of Dan" (May 18, 1897)
"The Return of Dick Weemins" (July 1897)
"The Suicide of Kiaros" (September 1897)
"A Shadow Cast Before" (December 1897)

"John" (June 24, 1898)
"The Mating Day" (September 1898)
"Aunt Hulda's Good Time" (October 26, 1899)
"The Loveridge Burglary" (January 1900)
"The Bad Man" (February 1901)
"The Ryl of the Lilies" (April 21, 1901)
"The King Who Changed His Mind" (1901)
"The Runaway Shadows or A Trick of Jack Frost" (June 5, 1901)
"(The Strange Adventures of) An Easter Egg" (March 29, 1902)
"Chrome Yellow" (1904, Unpublished)
"Mr. Rumple's Chill" (1904)
"Bess of the Movies" (1904)
"The Diamondback" (1904)
"A Kidnapped Santa Claus" (December 1904)
"The Woggle-Bug Book: The Unique Adventures of the Woggle-Bug" (January 12, 1905)
"Nelebel's Fairyland" (June 1905)
"Jack Burgitt's Honor" (August 1, 1905)
"The Tiger's Eye: A Jungle Fairy Tale" (1905)
"The Yellow Ryl" (1906)
"The Witchcraft of Mary–Marie" (1908)
"The Man-Fairy" (December 1910)
"Juggerjook" (December 1910)
"The Tramp and the Baby" (October 1911)
"Bessie's Fairy Tale" (December 1911)
"Aunt 'Phroney's Boy" (December 1912)
"The Littlest Giant—An Oz Story" (1918)
"An Oz Book" (1919)

As Edith Van Dyne:
Aunt Jane's Nieces (1906)
Aunt Jane's Nieces Abroad (1907)
Aunt Jane's Nieces at Millville (1908)
Aunt Jane's Nieces at Work (1909)
Aunt Jane's Nieces in Society (1910)
Aunt Jane's Nieces and Uncle John (1911)
The Flying Girl (1911)
Aunt Jane's Nieces on Vacation (1912)
The Flying Girl and Her Chum (1912)
Aunt Jane's Nieces on the Ranch (1913)
Aunt Jane's Nieces Out West (1914)
Aunt Jane's Nieces in the Red Cross (1915, revised and republished in 1918)
Mary Louise (1916)
Mary Louise in the Country (1916)
Mary Louise Solves a Mystery (1917)
Mary Louise and the Liberty Girls (1918)
Mary Louise Adopts a Soldier (1919; largely ghostwritten based on a fragment by Baum)

As Floyd Akers
The Boy Fortune Hunters in Alaska (1906)

The Boy Fortune Hunters in Panama (1907)
The Boy Fortune Hunters in Egypt (1908)
The Boy Fortune Hunters in China (1909)
The Boy Fortune Hunters in Yucatan (1910)
The Boy Fortune Hunters in the South Seas (1911)

As Schuyler Staunton
The Fate of a Crown (1905)
Daughters of Destiny (1906)

As John Estes Cooke
Tamawaca Folks: A Summer Comedy (1907)

As Suzanne Metcalf
Annabel, A Novel for Young Folk (1906)

As Laura Bancroft
The Twinkle Tales (1906)
Policeman Bluejay (1907)

Anonymous
The Last Egyptian: A Romance of the Nile (1908)

Miscellanea
Baum's Complete Stamp Dealer's Directory (1873)
The Book of the Hamburgs (poultry guide, 1886)
Our Landlady (newspaper stories, 1890–1891)
The Art of Decorating Dry Goods Windows and Interiors (trade publication, 1900)
L. Frank Baum's Juvenile Speaker (or Baum's Own Book for Children) (1910)

Plays and Adaptations
The Mackrummins (lost play, 1882)
The Maid of Arran (play, 1882)
Matches (lost play, 1882)
Kilmourne, or O'Connor's Dream (lost? play, opened April 4, 1883)
The Queen of Killarney (lost? play, 1883)
The Songs of Father Goose (Father Goose set to music by Alberta N. Hall Burton, 1900)
"The Maid of Athens: A College Fantasy" (play treatment, 1903; with Emerson Hough)
"The King of Gee-Whiz" (play treatment, February 1905, with Emerson Hough)
Mortal for an Hour or The Fairy Prince or Prince Marvel (play, 1909)
The Pipes O' Pan (play, 1909, with George Scarborough; only the first act was ever completed)
King Bud of Noland, or The Magic Cloak (musical play, 1913)
Stagecraft, or, The Adventures of a Strictly Moral Man (musical play, 1914)
Prince Silverwings (long term project with Edith Ogden Harrison; worked on as late as 1915)

The Uplift of Lucifer, or Raising Hell: An Allegorical Squazosh (musical play, 1915)
Blackbird Cottages: The Uplifters' Minstrels (musical play, 1916)
The Orpheus Road Show: A Paraphrastic Compendium of Mirth (musical play, 1917)

www.ingramcontent.com/pod-product-compliance
Lightning Source LLC
Chambersburg PA
CBHW061451170626
46811CB00004B/1456